PRINCESS OF FLAMES AND FATE

ARACELI'S BLADE
BOOK TWO

EMBER JOHNSON

CURSEBREAKER BOOKS

PRAISE FOR DAUGHTER OF SHADOWS AND ASH

This book was a page-turning adventure that I could not get enough of.

— AMAZON REVIEWER

I was so invested by the end of the book I was on the edge of my seat, and almost yelling when it ended!

— AMAZON REVIEWER

This book gave me everything I love in a fantasy... It's one of those stories that stays with you even after you've turned the last page.

— GOODREADS REVIEWER

To the ones who healed after walking through flames barefoot.

PLAYLIST

IN NO PARTICULAR ORDER

Sweet and dark - Miles Hardt

Is it a sin - John michael howell

The prophecy - Taylor swift

Bow (slowed) - Reyn Hartley

Hero - David kushner

Thorns and roses - Jazz Davis & olivia evans

Iris - Jada facer

mess it up - Gracie abrams

Something in the orange - our last night

Shipwreck - Letdown.

Take aim - Sleep token

We can't be friends (wait for your love) acoustic - Jada facer

Young and beautiful (DH orchestral) - Lana del rey

Chasing shadows - Alex warren

Letdown - Letdown.

Follow you - bring me the horizon

Lovely - Lauren babic & seraphim

Emergence - Sleep token

Tidal wave - our last night

Wait - seafret

Peacefield - Ghost

The water is fine - Chloe ament

Version of me - our last night

When the night is over - Lord huron

The new me - Thomas day

In the dark - bring me the horizon

Italy - Reyn hartley

Sweet oblivion - David kushner

Just my soul responding - Amber rush

Bad blood - seafret

I wanna get to heaven - David kushner

Where do we go from here - Amber rush

Glass Castle - Jazz Davis

Middle of the night - our last night

CONTENT WARNING

Princess of Flames and Fate may include the following graphic scenes and difficult topics intended for ages 18+. Please review before proceeding.

Death/murder, suggested rape/sexual assault, drowning, attempted murder, perceived infidelity, deaths of loved ones, abandonment, torture, kidnapping, depression, grief, and other potentially sensitive topics.

ARACELI
THE LOST ISLES
THE WITCH'S COTTAGE
ESMERAY
LUMI COVE
CHERMONA
OAKSTON
WILLOWBROOK
SOUOAK
BRIARWOOD
THE GREAT WOODS
THE ASSASSIN'S GUILD
SAINTS LANDING
BRIDGEDALE
EPHERINIA
SUNNEVA
N

CONTENTS

DAUGHTER OF SHADOWS AND ASH RECAP

Alora's journey of revenge began the night she lost her grandmother and fiancé, her childhood love Maël, after mercenaries raided her village. In a moment of rage and despair, her newly minted powers burst from her, surrounding her and their enemies in darkness before a blazing white flame took everything.

Only, the men got away.

She devoted her life to hunting them down, and she did so successfully until it came to the final one, Captain Johan. When she crossed paths with the assassin master, she makes a bargain to work alongside them using her shadow magic and they would help her find Johan.

Years later, she finally found the wretched man once again, only for him to slip away. She spent that night drinking her disappointment away, ultimately landing her in bed with a stranger.

When she's sent on an assignment that brings her closer to Johan and the crown, she realized that stranger was no mere guard, but the prince of Sunneva. After fulfilling the king's assessment, it's announced that she is to be married to the prince, her fated mate.

Alora and Oryn found middle ground and moved forward with the marriage only for him to be sent away the next morning. It's at that time that disaster struck, Alora is taken prisoner and unwillingly became the subject to the experiments of the Alchemist, a madman obsessed with harnessing her magic via her blood. In a last ditch effort of escape, Alora was able to unleash her wrath, only to be consumed by burnout before she could taste freedom.

CHAPTER 1

Fire licked my skin as tongues of flame danced around me. Smoke choked the air, my throat raw from the lack of clean oxygen. Screams echoed around me as men, women, and children used every avenue to escape. The inferno cast the only light on this pitch-black night. The heat blistered my lungs with each breath, and the crackling flames drowned out everything but the primal terror in those desperate screams. Death danced in the shadows between buildings, waiting to claim those too slow to escape.

"There you are, Little Hunter." I turned to confront my lost love, Maël. A sword protruded from his abdomen, blood spreading across his clothing. His face and arms were littered with bruises and scratches. "Finally remembered me after all this time. Crawling back now that your mate threw you away."

"No," my voice was scratchy with the plea that escaped, "I never forgot you."

"Save your pathetic lies, you were all too happy to wed him. You were supposed to be mine." His words cut like knives. The kind man I used to know had twisted into something wrathful. Even during the most trying days in our village, I'd never seen this display of fury mar his features.

I wanted to rush to him, comfort him, but my body wouldn't yield to my commands. The only movements within my grasp were my words.

"I'm sorry, Maël," hot tears traced paths down my face, "I was unable to help it, the bond—it made it impossible not to fall under his spell. But all I wanted was to save you."

His head tilted. "Save me? You fucking killed me."

His words struck with the force of an axe as the surrounding scene shifted. The once burgundy and orange flames transformed into a brilliant white. I finally could move my hands, only to see them coated with that same devastating light. My fire. I checked on Maël, only to see, with horror, that the fire had consumed him. No matter how hard I tried, I lacked the power to influence the flames. They devoured him and everything around us. A scream tore from me, begging me to stop. My heart shattered as I watched my power consume the man I loved, my fingers clawing at my chest as if I could rip out the magic that betrayed me. The white flames danced across his skin like a lover's caress, a mockery of the tender touches we'd never share again.

I JOLTED AWAKE. No blood. No ash. Just the phantom scent of death clinging to my memories.

Reality's return weakened the nightmare's grasp, washing away the hellish vision.

My hands trembled against the mattress, my heart thundered to a point where my ragged breathing was unheard.

The crisp scent of fresh rain and heady earth whispered through the air.

My fingers tangled into unfamiliar satin sheets. Every breath sent daggers through my ribs, my body a map of pain.

The unfamiliar ornate ceiling loomed above me, nothing like my chambers in Sunneva's golden palace with their large golden globes. Dark stone covered the room, a night sky swirling with shades of indigo and violet reminded me of the many nights I spent looking up into the dark heavens, willing the gods to enlighten me about their reasons. Pleading for them to shift fate in my favor, even if just for a moment.

Morning light crept through heavy silver curtains while I assessed my prison - or sanctuary.

This wasn't Sunneva, nor the darkness of that cursed dungeon.

A gentle snore caught my attention.

A mountain of a man was curled impossibly small in a plush armchair beside my bed.

A short beard hugged a strong jawline. Something about him tugged at my memory, but his dark features remained unfamiliar.

If he meant to harm me, he was failing spectacularly at playing guard.

The chamber door groaned on its hinges as a tall figure slipped through.

Kyler approached, his usual arrogant stride absent. Dark circles shadowed his eyes, his clothes rumpled as if he'd slept in them.

"You're awake." He crossed to my bedside, lifting a cup to place it carefully in my hands with a gentle nod.

My arms trembled with the effort of lifting the cup, but the cool water was a blessing against my parched throat.

"We weren't sure you'd make it." His voice cracked on the last word.

"We?" The word scraped past my lips like broken glass.

Kyler kicked the massive figure in the chair's boot. "Rasher and I found you. Seems you two made quite the pair in those cells."

"What happened?"

He gave me an inquisitive look. "I hoped you could tell me. The day Oryn left for the war front, Magnus burst into my quarters, frantic about your disappearance and signs of struggle in your room.

We searched for weeks until a guard mentioned a new prisoner in the dungeons. When I went to investigate, the place was ablaze. You were fighting someone until..." He took a deep breath, his eyes haunted by the memory. "Until you weren't. I barely got you out before the flames claimed everything."

"The most trusted man in the prince's guard finds me in the dungeon and doesn't question why? Just sweeps in to save me as if I were a damsel in distress?"

A man, a part of the very guards who imprisoned me, now lets me roam free. Something about this doesn't add up.

He rocks back on his heels, gaze fixed on the floor, "Oryn wouldn't have allied with you if you deserved that cell. After what this fool told me about what he witnessed... no one deserves that kind of treatment."

His eyes meet mine, brimming with unwanted pity.

"Though you are technically a damsel. And nearly burning yourself out counts as distress, wouldn't you say?"

A slight smile touched his lips after stating the fact; his smug satisfaction filled the room. A dangerous glint danced in his eyes as he leaned against the bedpost, preening. It made me want to stab him. His account of what he witnessed brings the memories of my time with the Alchemist crashing back - the feel of the grimy cell floor beneath my skin, the putrid stench of mold and decay that clung to the damp stone walls, the constant drip of water that marked time in endless darkness. The bitter taste of Oryn's betrayal lingered on my tongue... I felt for the thread that binds me to him, our connection still sealed in my mind. A brush of warmth told me Maël was still here. My heart clenched with feeling his presence, the one constant in my life that hadn't betrayed me yet.

Lost in the depths of memory, I jerked back to the present.

Kyler's worried frown met my eyes as I also saw a familiar pair of brown eyes staring back at me. They had been my only light in the darkness of our shared prison. His trimmed beard replaced the matted mess from our imprisonment. But those eyes, now that he's awake - I would know them anywhere. Whatever crime landed him in that cell meant nothing now.

After all, my own hands weren't exactly clean.

My gaze snapped back to Kyler, my face hardening as survival's bitter relief twisted into rage at the memory of how I ended up in that hell.

The question clawed its way up my throat. "Does Oryn know I'm here?"

"No. I planned to intercept him on his return to the castle tonight. But given the mysterious circumstances of your imprisonment, the castle isn't safe. I brought you here to heal while we unravel this mess."

"The royal family is more involved in what happened than you would think." My hands clutched the thick blanket on my lap. "If you truly value my safety, you will not inform him you've found me or know where I am."

He gave me a searching look. "You're his mate, he would never..."

"You don't know what happened," I snarled. How dare he declare what Oryn would or wouldn't do!? I thought he wouldn't turn his back on me and that only landed me inside a cold, dark cell. A personal pincushion for a maniac.

Rasher rose to his feet with a throat-clearing rumble. I hadn't thought it possible, but he towered over both Kyler and Oryn. He moved to the bedside in less than a step, positioning himself between Kyler and me like a living shield. Brown eyes met my own as he looked down, searching my face. Silently, I pleaded for him to see reason with my plight. The subtle nod made my shoulders drop with relief as he turned to Oryn's friend.

"Letting him know could alert those responsible," Rasher warned, eyes locked on Kyler. His unease intensified by the second, his eyes flitting between us. "You'll only succeed in putting her in danger once again."

After a long moment, Kyler released a heavy breath and shook his head. "Fine. We'll keep this quiet for now." His dark eyes locked onto mine. "But I expect the full story eventually, Lady Alora. Every detail matters if we're to get to the bottom of it."

"We'll see." I crossed my arms. "How long has it been since I was taken?"

Kyler scrubbed his jaw. "Several weeks until we heard that tip. Your wedding took place at the end of the fall. It's now nearing the end of winter."

Months. I spent months being tortured by that maniac. The time I had lost to darkness far exceeded what I assumed. It felt like mere days, long, brutal days. How could I have lost all of that time with no awareness?

"Where are we?"

"We brought you to Esmeray," Rasher answered. He gave me an odd look and then let his eyes drift towards Kyler. "Home was the safest place to bring you."

Home? I wasn't surprised that Rasher came from here, but Kyler's presence shocked me. Why would someone from Esmeray help Sunneva fight his own people?

My fingers dug into my arms as I studied Kyler with newfound wariness. One of the highest ranking fae in Sunneva's guard is a son of Esmeray - every certainty I had about him crumbled like frost in sunlight.

I didn't have time to interrogate Kyler as a maid bustled in carrying a tray of steaming tea and fresh bandages. "My lady, thank the gods. Let's get you cleaned up and changed."

The maid helped me sit up. Pain lanced through my muscles like shards of glass, the punishment for being so far away from my soulmate.

"Get dressed." Kyler's voice hardened to steel. "We've been requested for an audience."

"An audience with whom?"

"Seems the queen is eager to meet her newest guest." Kyler waved his hand in a gesture to hurry as he and Rasher stepped out of the room, whispering to each other like shadows trading secrets. The maid scrambled to help me up and into decent clothes. Relief flooded through me at the sight of leather pants and a simple blouse. Beautiful boots lay before me, and my breath caught at their perfection. Intricate stitches adorned the black leather up the sides. Though I may have lost my weapons and belongings in Sunneva, these boots will make a worthy beginning.

CHAPTER 2

The rhythmic thumps of our boots echoed through the hallways as I followed Kyler to the throne room. The Esmeraean castle is a stark contrast to the one that stands in Sunneva. In contrast to the first, which shone like the sun, this one seemed to be constructed from heavy, dark stone. Black as night, with veins of silver running through it like captured lightning.

Attendees and guards passed by us without a second thought some pointed ears, but not all, along with maids who carried trays and linens. Some of the men we passed with swords strapped to their sides were human. This was wholly different than Sunneva with their human servants and their fae knights. Always favoring the strongest, they exploited the weakest for any potential gain. Luella was happiest while alone with me in my rooms or in the library, but Miss Gregoria never hesitated to come down on her. Around others, her once sweet smile turned into a solemn shield.

Everyone here seemed...happy. It wasn't as if they walked around with grins plastered on their faces. No, everyone seemed to acknowledge each other with mutual respect, their heads held high with pride instead of downward to avoid the ire of a noble.

I tried to memorize the path—left, right, straight, then left again —but another turn caused me to get lost. Each corridor looked identical to the last.

"If you leave me alone in this place, I'll never find my way out," I muttered.

Kyler glanced over his shoulder, his dark eyes assessing me. "Is that a request for me to abandon you, or a warning not to?"

"Very funny." I quickened my pace, feeling Rasher right on my heels with his long strides. "So what's she like? Your queen?"

"Complicated."

I hear a snort from behind, but Rasher chooses not to elaborate.

"That's helpful."

"I wasn't trying to be helpful." The corner of Kyler's mouth twitched. "I was being honest."

We approached a set of imposing double doors, each carved with intricate designs that seemed to shift in the dim light. Two guards stood at attention, their faces impassive beneath their helmets.

"Any last pieces of advice?" I whispered.

Kyler paused, turning to face me fully. "Don't lie. She'll know. Don't volunteer information she doesn't ask for. And whatever you do, don't mention—"

The doors swung open before he could finish, revealing a cavernous throne room that seemed to stretch into infinity. Black marble floors reflected the hundreds of floating lights that hovered near the vaulted ceiling. And at the far end, seated upon a throne that appeared to be carved from a single massive crystal, was the Queen of Esmeray.

"Breathe," Kyler murmured beside me. "And try not to stare."

Too late. I was already staring.

I stood frozen at the threshold, taking in the sight before me. The Queen of Esmeray didn't just sit on her throne—she commanded it. Her hair was the color of the bright rubies that adorned many of the Sunnevean ladies, braided intricately with black gems that caught the light. Her skin held the same pallor as fresh snow, with eyes so dark they appeared endless.

The throne room fell into hushed silence as we approached. My heartbeat thundered in my ears, drowning out even the soft click of our boots against the marble floor. The distance to the throne seemed endless, giving me far too much time to notice the few guards in attendance tracking our progress.

Kyler moved with the serene confidence of a noble returning home. Rasher kept a respectful distance behind us, his presence a steady comfort.

The queen watched our approach with a stillness that reminded me of a predator. No fidgeting, no unnecessary movement—just those dark, unfathomable eyes taking in every detail.

When we reached the appropriate distance from the throne, Kyler bowed deeply. I followed his lead, though my movements seemed stiff and unpracticed.

"Your Majesty," Kyler greeted, his voice carrying across the chamber. "May I present Lady Alora of Sunneva."

"Queen Wynaria," Rasher greeted from behind us.

The queen's gaze shifted fully to me, and I felt a chill race down my spine. Her expression remained neutral, yet I sensed her measuring me, weighing my worth with each passing second.

"Rise," she commanded, her voice surprisingly melodic despite its authority.

I straightened, fighting the urge to fidget under her scrutiny.

"So this is the one who's caused such a stir." The queen leaned forward slightly, her braided ruby hair catching the light. "I've heard many things about you, Alora Satori."

My throat went dry at the use of my full name. "I hope not all terrible, Your Majesty."

A flicker of something—amusement—crossed her face. "That depends entirely on who's doing the telling, little bird."

She rose from her throne in one fluid motion, descending the three steps that elevated her position. Even standing before me, she maintained her regal bearing, tall and imposing.

"You've traveled far from your home, Princess of the Sun." She circled me slowly, her movements deliberate. "And left quite the trail of chaos in your wake."

I stayed still, unsure if I should respond.

"Tell me, princess, what am I to do with you?"

I met her gaze steadily. "That depends on what you want from me, Your Majesty."

Another laugh, shorter this time. "Direct. I understand why my son is intrigued. I bet the southern king just *loves* you."

Son? I fought to keep my expression neutral as I glanced at Kyler, whose face had gone carefully blank.

The queen noticed our exchange and smiled, sharp and held no warmth. "Oh, did he not mention that detail? Our prince has always kept his secrets."

My mind reeled at the revelation. Kyler—a prince? The pieces started clicking into place: his commanding presence, the way the guards deferred to him, his intimate knowledge of both courts.

"You seem surprised, princess." The queen's voice dripped with amusement. "Did you think he was merely another soldier?"

"I'm not sure what I thought," venom taints each careful word as I stare him down. How did I miss this? The Esmerean prince inside the Sunnevean castle? Best friends with the prince while his people were slaughtered every day?

Kyler shifted beside me, a barely perceptible movement. Was that tension in his shoulders, or something else?

"Secrets upon secrets." The queen descended the last steps between us. Up close, her beauty was even more striking—and more terrible. "Yet I believe you have your own. Secrets, that is."

Ice crawled up my spine. There were many secrets hidden in the shadows, most of which would see my head removed from my body.

"Everyone carries their own burdens," I said, careful to keep my face neutral, "and I am no exception."

The queen stopped before me, assessing me once again before turning her gaze to her son.

"You've chosen an interesting companion, my son. Tell me, what are you hoping to gain, Death's Wraith?"

CHAPTER 3

Kyler's sharp intake of breath cut through the tension like a
blade. His dark eyes locked onto mine, no longer carefully
neutral but filled with a storm of emotions—recognition,
betrayal, and something darker.

"Death's Wraith." His voice was barely above a whisper, but it
carried the weight of years of pursuit. "All this time..."

Despite my racing heart, I maintained a neutral expression. The
one he'd been chasing, the shadow that slipped through his fingers
time and again—had been off marrying his friend.

"This whole time..." The surrounding temperature plummeted.
Frost crackled across the floor, spreading from where he stood. "I've
searched every dark alley day and night and you're telling me all I
had to do was return to court and she would be right in front of me?"
His tone dripped with disdain. "Tell me, is your husband aware he's
bound himself to a criminal?"

I felt immense guilt on our wedding day, knowing Oryn barely
knew me as he vowed his love. But now, after what he did, that guilt
doesn't weigh as heavily anymore. Fate made us two halves of one
soul. I guess a murderer and a torturer do belong together.

"I don't believe Prince Oryn cared about anything other than using me for his own agenda." My voice is low with warning.

Kyler's eyes narrowed on me. "Somehow I doubt that, considering the numerous reports I've received of your slaughters in Sunneva." I didn't back away from his advance, even as ice crystals formed in the air between us.

"You doubt that, yet you've seen firsthand what Sunneva is capable of, what they do to their prisoners." I can't resist a glance at Rasher, who's stood off to the side, a quiet sentinel. "I can assure you, anyone who died by my hand deserved it tenfold."

"And that gives you the right to be judge, jury, and executioner?" His words came out in frozen puffs of air.

He gazed at me, his eyes searching for something—perhaps answers, or the slightest hint of remorse. He wouldn't find any. That part of me resolved itself after my first few missions. Every life I'd taken had been necessary, each death a step toward preventing countless others from suffering a fate they didn't deserve.

"They were monsters. I was simply the assigned exterminator." I lifted my chin.

"The only monster in existence is you!" He roared, pacing away, his hands fisted at his sides.

"While you got cozy with your life in the southern court, I removed those who threatened your people. I've liberated buildings full of your subjects who were being trafficked. Tell me, Prince Kyler," the title a sneer, "what have you done to protect your people? Because I have done whatever was asked."

The queen's laughter rang out, sharp and delighted. "Oh, this is better than I could have hoped. My son, unknowingly harboring the very assassin he's been hunting."

Kyler's jaw clenched. "You knew."

"Of course I knew." She waved a hand dismissively. "I've known since the moment you brought her here. Though convenient, I've been waiting to meet the one and only Death's Wraith."

That made him pause. Though anger was apparent on his face, his eyes shone with confusion.

The queen's eyes gleamed with secrets as she circled us. "Quite the conundrum, really. Protecting the life of your sworn enemy. Or is she? Her master has quite the moral compass despite her line of work. Maybe she's instilled that same sense into her heir. Speaking of Vanya, she sends her regards."

My blood turned to ice. "You know Vanya?"

"Oh, darling. Who do you think has financed all of your assignments?" She traced a finger along the back of her throne. "While King Aurelius continued to slaughter our villages near the woods, his people have also stolen women and children and brought them across that very border you claim I have no jurisdiction." She looks pointedly at Kyler. "I don't care if it's an entirely different realm. I will not leave my people to suffer. The war between Sunneva and Esmeray has grown... complicated. Hiding their missing princess won't improve the situation."

"That's not—"

"Hush." She cut me off with a wave. "I will not give that smug bastard an excuse to justify this scrimmage even further." I could feel my heart racing with the thought of being forced to return, chained and at the whims of whatever experiments Oryn and his father had in store for me. "If the king presses the matter publicly, we can use that to prevent more damage. But my kindness has a cost."

My eyebrow quirked up, "and what would that cost be?"

"I want to see what you're truly capable of," she mused as she sits upon her throne once again. "The people need a sword, and you've proven quite capable with a blade. Join our cause to end this nonsense with the south."

I crossed my arms. "I'm not anyone's weapon."

"Let fate decide what you are and what you are not." The queen's smile held no warmth. "You will journey up the mountain and face the witch who speaks to Fate. You will claim your destiny."

"And if I refuse?"

"Then you forfeit my protection and you will be delivered to that gaudy palace with a pretty golden bow faster than you can blink." She turned to Kyler. "She's officially your charge. You will accompany her."

"No." Kyler stepped forward. "Mother, you can't be serious. She's a murderer, a traitor—"

He's one to talk about being a traitor, but I don't voice my thoughts.

"I am your queen before I am your mother." Steel entered her voice. "This is not a request. And I expect you to further her training while she's in your care."

Kyler's jaw tightened. The temperature dropped further, and frost spread across the marble floor. The queen cut him a look at his icy display.

Realizing I had no other choice, I nodded.

"Meet Rasher at dawn." He spat the words like poison and stomped out of the grand hall without another word.

Rasher looked at me with sympathy as he motioned for me to follow him. The sound of the queen's amusement chimed in the air as we left, opposite the direction of the angry prince. This witch in the mountains felt like another test, another game where I wasn't told all the rules. This time, I had a partner that would love to see me dead before spending another moment with me.

Perfect.

CHAPTER 4

I rose before dawn, my mind still aching from yesterday's revelations. The prince's cold fury had followed me into my dreams, turning my sleep restless and shallow. Now I faced whatever torture I was sure Kyler arranged with Rasher. As kind as the big man was to me, I knew his allegiance was with his prince.

Thankfully, the trek was simple thanks to some of the guards posted near my room. The training yard was empty when I arrived, save for Rasher's hulking form. He stood with his back to me, arranging various weapons on a wooden table.

"You're early," he said without turning around.

"Couldn't sleep." I approached, keeping my footsteps silent out of habit. "Being branded a murderer and a monster tends to do that."

Rasher finally turned, scratching his dark facial hair in thought. His eyes held none of Kyler's malice, just a quiet assessment.

"I cannot judge your actions, as I have faced many difficult choices myself. While the prince is very strategic, sometimes he's a bit too reactive to look at the whole picture... or person."

I lifted a wood sword from the selection, testing the weight of the wooden handle, shifting it in my hand and recalling a time long, long ago when I would smack Maël with a similar one.

I had you on your back more times than I can count. Don't go rewriting history.

If I were to rewrite anything, it would be to save you.

The warmth of Maël's presence filled my mind, giving me enough ease to bring clarity.

"And do you," Forced to look up to meet Rasher's eyes, his height dwarfing mine, "look at the whole person?"

He was quiet for a moment. "I'm looking forward to seeing what Death's Wraith is really like." He moved into a fighting stance.

I mirrored his stance, muscles remembering years of training. When he lunged, I was ready. I sidestepped his attack, countering with a swift strike that he barely blocked. Surprise flickered in his eyes.

A wicked grin spread across my face. "I'll try not to maim you too badly."

Rasher let out a snort before lunging again, my taunt costing me a knick to my arm.

We danced across the yard, wooden swords clacking in the dawn light. I anticipated his movements, reading the subtle shifts in his weight, the tension in his shoulders before each strike. When he aimed high, I went low. When he feinted left, I was already moving right. He was good, better than me, despite our parrying. I relied on speed to keep out of his way, but I knew if he were to land a real hit, I'd be knocked out for sure.

"Enough." Rasher lowered his sword, breathing hard. "You've had proper training."

"Proper is a loose term." I went to the table and picked up a gleaming dagger that caught my eye. The small blade was a familiar feeling in my palm as I shifted and launched it to the target just behind the big guy, narrowly missing him. His eyes widened as the blade embedded into the cork, the thump following shortly after.

My new trainer narrowed his eyes at my antics and pointed toward a target at the far end of the yard. "Bow next." He barked.

The bow felt like an extension of my arm. I nocked an arrow, drew back, and released in one fluid motion. The arrow struck dead center. The next five followed, clustering so tightly around the first that the fletching touched.

"Is there anything you're not skillful with, or is her mighty assassin-ness flawless in every way?"

I gingerly set the bow back down on the table and shirked the quiver of arrows. "Axes aren't really my forte."

He scoffed and waved me off. "With your size, they're a death sentence. You're better off using your bare hands. No, we won't waste any time there. Let's work with your shadows. I caught a glimpse of them the night we... escaped. It's a useful power for an assassin."

"It is indeed." I closed my eyes, reaching for the darkness that lived within me. It responded eagerly, curling around my fingers like smoke. I sent it spiraling toward the targets, weaving it between them, making it dance and twist to my will.

"Good control," Rasher muttered. "What else can you do?"

I shot him a wink before I encased myself in shadow, the very thing that likely led to my moniker.

It was hard to decipher what he was thinking. His eyes were focused and assessing, but there seemed to be something more that I couldn't quite grasp. I walked backwards into the shade, going nearly invisible. I watched his eyes as I began to circle him. By the time I ended up on his right, I could tell he couldn't track me. His eyes never left the spot which I entered. I popped back into the sunlight, but the brute didn't startle.

"Let's see your fire now."

My confidence faltered. I'd never been able to control it, never truly cared to. All it did was demolish everything in its path. I pushed the memories that clung so tight to the power aside, the sight of my village burning, the putrid smell of the dungeon where I was held prisoner, and tried to connect to the wild power, pulling the heat to my palms. A small flame flickered to life, dancing across my fingers without burning. I tried to shape it, to direct it towards the waiting target.

The flame surged suddenly, exploding outward in a wave that scorched the ground and sent Rasher diving for cover.

"Shit." Fire licked up my arms, hungry and wild. The flames roared higher, feeding off my panic. I stumbled back, trying to contain it, but the inferno only grew.

"Get back!" I screamed as the fire surged outward in waves. The heat seared my skin, but didn't burn - a small mercy.

A blast of icy air cut through the flames. Kyler stood at the edge of the training yard, frost crackling around his outstretched hands. His dark eyes met mine with a mix of fury and something else I couldn't name.

"What in the seven hells were you thinking?" He stalked forward, ice spreading beneath his feet. "You could have killed someone."

"I didn't mean—" The words died in my throat as another surge of fire burst from my palms.

Kyler moved faster than thought, ice meeting fire in a hiss of steam. His powers wrapped around mine, containing, cooling, until the flames finally sputtered out.

"This is exactly why you need proper training." His voice was winter-cold. "Oryn could help-"

"No." The word came out sharp as a blade. "I won't go to him."

"He's the only other fire wielder who could—"

"He knew." My hands shook. "He knew I was in that dungeon and did nothing."

Kyler went still. "What?"

"Your best friend," I spat the words, "watched me rot in chains for months and never lifted a finger to help."

The temperature dropped further, frost crystallizing in the air between us. Kyler's face had gone blank, unreadable.

"We leave for the witch at dawn," he said finally, voice flat. "Try not to burn anything else down before then."

He turned and strode away, leaving me standing in a circle of scorched earth. Rasher gave me a long look before following.

I stared at my trembling hands, wondering if I was more monster than person after all...

CHAPTER 5

We left the castle gates the next morning, with the sky softly painted pink by the dawn. The tension between Kyler and me hung in the air as thick as fog, neither of us speaking a word. Rasher trailed behind, attempting casual conversation that died quickly in the heavy silence. Every sway of my horse's steps made me think of my own. I hoped Raven was still being well cared for. Maybe I could get a message to Lucas to recover him for me. He was the best thief in the land, and I had no doubts about his ability to do it. Though, whether Raven would intimidate him... well, that was an entirely different issue.

Several days into our journey, wisps of smoke caught my attention, rising lazily above the treeline. The sound of music and laughter drifted through the branches, carried on the spring breeze.

"We should check it out," Rasher said, already veering his horse toward the noise. "Could be trouble."

"We don't have time for distractions." Kyler's jaw clenched.

I rolled my eyes. "Two against one, Your Highness."

Kyler gave me a sharp look as I urged my horse onward, following Rasher on his chestnut steed. I returned his stare with an indifferent one of my own until he fell behind. We soon arrived at what Rasher called Lumi Cove.

The village square burst with color and life. Flower garlands draped between buildings, bright ribbons fluttered in the wind. Villagers danced in circles, celebrating winter's end with wild abandon. The scent of sweet pastries made my mouth water.

"I'll grab us some food," Rasher announced, vanishing into the crowd before we voiced our objections.

Kyler and I dismounted our horses, tying them up to a nearby post along with Rasher's. After watering the horses, we took in the surrounding sight. We stood awkwardly apart, watching children dash past, throwing handfuls of flower petals. A tiny girl with missing front teeth tugged at my sleeve, offering a crown of fresh-picked wildflowers. As I knelt to let her place it on my head, I caught Kyler's expression softening for just a moment. Instantly, the moment vanished, replaced by the impassive mask he'd worn since our audience with the queen. Without a word, he began walking into the fray, leaving me to stumble behind him like a lovesick pup.

Are you in love with him? I thought you only loved the golden one. Maël's voice caressed my mind.

I don't love either of them. Kyler is a traitor to his people and Oryn betrayed me. They would be a perfect match.

Lor, I can't imagine your mate would've arranged for your torture. Don't you think you're rushing to conclusions without any proof?

Even my own hallucinations questioned whether Oryn bore the blame for my captivity in his dungeon. It seemed everyone felt Ryn was infallible; my suggestion that he might act in such a manner appeared insane to them. But if he wouldn't, why did the Alchemist insinuate he was? The way he told it, you'd assume Oryn was the very mastermind behind that.

I'm sure the torture I suffered proves my point.

Alora, I'm not trying to brush off what you went through. I was unable to reach you when you were there. I wish I could've been by your side. But

I've seen how Oryn interacts with you. I've heard his thoughts and experienced his feelings towards you. Believe someone who would've given their life for you. It seems unlikely to me that he's a talented enough actor to have fabricated all of that.

But you did give your life for mine. My retort came off harshly, but I felt my anger rise. *You're gone because of me. It's all my fault and I still haven't killed the one responsible. I would've thought you of all people would've been on my side.*

I still didn't understand how Maël was able to talk to me and seem tangible to me in my thoughts, but I tried to shove him away from the forefront of my mind. He seemed to receive the hint and slinked back to one of the dark corners where he often disappeared. Good, now I was able to focus on the merriment around me instead of the warring feelings in my mind.

The musicians struck up a new tune, and suddenly Kyler and I were pushed together by the surging crowd. His hands caught my waist as I stumbled, steadying myself against his chest. The touch sent unexpected sparks racing across my skin. Just as quickly, he distances himself from me once again.

"We should…" he started.

I nodded, knowing he was looking for a way to exit. We continued to get jostled amongst the dancers. Pushed from behind, I toppled forward, bracing for impact with the hard dirt, but it never came. Kyler caught me in his arms, this time his hands not leaving my waist.

"Just until the song ends." He murmured. I wasn't sure if it was to console me or himself.

We joined the villagers in their revelry. Thankfully, Kyler was more than capable of leading someone as inexperienced as me. The memory of that mission with Lucas, where he abandoned me amidst the dancing, and that stranger I could barely forget, came back to me.

Each turn brought us face to face, something dangerous building in the space between us, his grip tightening. The dance drew us closer with each measure, his breath warming my cheek.

Someone bumped us toward a quiet alley, and my back hit the cool stone wall. Kyler's eyes dropped to my lips, his body caging mine. The world narrowed to just this moment, just us.

Until the crowd erupted in applause, shattering the spell.

He jerked away like I'd burned him. "This was a mistake. We should go find Rasher and continue on." Regret shone in his eyes and my stomach twisted sickening fast when I realized why.

"We should." I snapped. "Heaven forbid the precious prince of Esmeray sully himself with a murderer."

"You don't understand—"

"No, I understand perfectly. You don't trust me, just like I don't trust a traitor like you." The words tasted like poison, but I couldn't help but wield them.

"You know nothing about me or my position!"

"Well, that makes two of us!" I stormed off into the crowd, leaving him alone in the shadows.

CHAPTER 6

I stormed away from Kyler, fuming at his dismissal. The villagers' cheerful faces blurred as I pushed through the crowd, my mind replaying our almost kiss in the alley.

Rasher's broad frame suddenly appeared, waving a muscular arm to catch our attention. "There you two are!" he called over the noise. "I found the good stuff." He lifted a platter of food until it was in line with his chest, smiling proudly at his haul.

I nodded stiffly, grabbing a roll from the spoils. I refused to look at Kyler as he approached behind me.

"We should get moving if we want to make it up the mountain before nightfall."

Rasher grumbled, but a sharp look silenced him. The prince set the pace for this journey. Food be damned. As our footsteps pounded the dirt near our horses, the brawny man gave the remaining food to a nearby group of children, who gleefully ran off with it. Once I was back in my saddle, I observed the two men. Rasher looked intimidating being as tall as a horse and as wide as three men, but I've noticed he tends to be softer, at least when he doesn't have orders to kill you. I reminded myself that he, like me, was incarcerated.

Kyler presented a unique challenge. Righteous, proud, determined to do things his way. Every time we clashed, the gentle giant defended him, insisting there was more to him. I huffed to myself, thinking about the possibility he was a good man. A talented dancer, sure. But someone who fought for his enemy and saw kissing me as beneath him left a lot to be desired. And yet, when he had me against the wall...

I didn't bother finishing that thought as Kyler barked at me to move along as he ushered us away from the lively town, sight set north.

The steep mountain path wound endlessly upward, each turn revealing only more rocky terrain ahead. My legs burned with the effort, but I pushed on, determined not to show weakness.

The steepness of the path forced us to lead the horses by their reins. My boots slipped on loose stones, sending several tumbling down the mountainside. Before I could regain my balance, Kyler's hand caught my elbow without even looking back, steadying me.

I jerked away from his touch as if burned. "Surprised you didn't let the *murderer* off herself."

"I considered it." He deadpanned, clearly not in the mood for my snark.

Ahead of us, Rasher rolled his eyes so dramatically I could practically hear them rattling in his skull.

The wind whipped my cloak around my legs, making each step more difficult. Dark clouds gathered overhead, promising trouble.

A deep thunder rumbled in the distance, and Kyler muttered something about "poor timing."

"Sorry, the weather doesn't conform to your royal preferences," I snapped.

"Alright, that's enough," Rasher called back. "Let's take a break before you two kill each other or the storm drowns us."

We found shelter under a rocky outcropping just as the first drops began to fall. I sat as far from Kyler as possible, pressing myself against the cold stone wall.

The rain started falling in sheets, creating a watery curtain across the opening of our shelter. Rasher passed out dried meat and bread from his pack. Silence stretched uncomfortably between us as we ate.

Lightning flashed, illuminating our tense faces in harsh, white light. I stared at the ground, counting the seconds between thunder and lightning. The horses whinnied uneasily beneath a thick crop of trees near our shelter.

"So, Alora," Rasher said suddenly. "Tell me about your first kill."

A scoff escaped Kyler's lips at the question. "Really, Rasher? That's your idea of pleasant conversation?"

I shot Kyler a glare before answering. "I was sixteen. Just learning to hunt in the woods outside my village and hit a small doe with an arrow." I shrugged.

"I was talking about more than just a hunt," Rasher said, "but at some point, it's all the same."

"Yeah, I guess your bloodlust has to start from somewhere." Kyler spat out bitterly.

"Believe it or not, *your highness*, I didn't set out for this. At sixteen, it was just a deer. I was only feeding me and my grandmother. Not feeding a psychotic need to kill everything in sight." I sighed as I stretched my legs, looking ahead as the rain pelted down. "It's hard to recall," I lied, not wanting to divulge yet how I lost control of myself and decimated my own village in a fit of rage. "It was so long ago."

Rasher nodded understanding. "Sometimes our path chooses us."

I caught Kyler's expression flickering with something like doubt before he looked away.

"After I sought restitution for my family, it stopped looking so black and white," I continued. "There were so many being terrorized that killing those who were wrecking havoc seemed grayer and grayer until it didn't matter. It's a shame. The worst beasts in the land are simply corrupted people and fae."

Kyler's shoulders tensed. Without a word, he stood and walked to the edge of our shelter, his back rigid.

"I never killed anyone who didn't deserve it," I said, my voice rising. "Every life I took saved dozens more."

"Keep telling yourself that." Kyler's words cut through the air before he stalked out into the rain.

Rasher shifted closer, his colossal frame blocking some of the stiff wind. "Don't mind him. He forgets some of the decisions he's made along the way that are not so different."

I pulled my knees to my chest. "You understand, though, don't you? Sometimes, the only way to protect people is to eliminate the threat."

"I do." His voice was softer than I'd ever heard it. "That's why I tried to kill the King of Sunneva. He was destroying lives, tearing families apart. Sometimes one death can prevent countless others."

"Is that how you ended up in the dungeon?"

"It was." He scratched his dark beard, "on my prince's orders. But plans go astray and sometimes you need to sit in the dark to regroup for the next opportunity." Rasher's smile was kind. "I have faith that he'll come around to you soon. He needs a broader perspective, beyond his personal judgments. Just give him time."

"I'm not sure I care if he does," I whispered.

Rasher's laugh rumbled like distant thunder. "Sure you don't. Perhaps you shouldn't inform him. I would rather not listen to him whine about it for the rest of our trip."

I couldn't help but smile. Despite everything, I'd found an unlikely friend in this gentle giant. Someone who understood the weight of necessary evils.

The night settled around us like a heavy blanket. I found a spot near the edge of our camp that was still dry. The sky was clear enough now to gaze up at the stars scattered across the inky sky.

Lor. Maël's voice whispered in my mind, warm and familiar. *Be careful up there.*

Always am, I thought back, *always am.*

That's the biggest lie you've ever told me. His mental laugh wrapped around me like an embrace.

I drifted off with a smile, his presence lingering until sleep took me.

Morning came too quickly. As Kyler and I prepared to make the final climb, Rasher pulled me aside.

"Remember, fate has a way of setting us on the right path, even when we think we're lost." He squeezed my shoulder. "I'll keep watch here. Just try not to kill him on your way up."

"Are you really going to leave me alone with him?"

"Someone has to stay with the horses." He waved me off. "It's a quick hike up. I'll see you back before the moon rises once again." He left me standing there to tend to the hungry steeds. A grunt from behind me made me turn towards the one person I'd rather not be alone with.

"The sooner you start moving, the sooner we can finish this nonsense."

After tossing and turning all night, I didn't bother gracing Kyler with a response as I began to follow him.

Our boots crunching on loose rock was the only sound during the silent uphill trek. Kyler walked ahead, his shoulders tense. Hours passed without a word said between us, though the prince still had his ways of telling me how put off he was to be here with me. I hadn't exactly signed up to travel for weeks in his presence. I'd rather travel with a rabid raccoon as a companion instead.

"Why are you really coming?" I asked, ducking under a low-hanging branch.

"The queen ordered me to see you here."

"You could've sent Rasher with me and you stay at the camp. You still would've seen to the journey."

"I have questions for the witch." He didn't look back. "Not everything revolves around you."

"Could've fooled me with how much you've been watching my every move."

He stopped so suddenly I almost ran into him. "Someone has to make sure you don't murder half the kingdom."

I stepped up, my face right below his as I met his glare, "Maybe if you would've dealt with the problem yourself, I wouldn't have had to slit the throats of so many." Storming ahead, I half expected him to drive a knife in my back. I was a bit surprised at the lack of stabbing, but the lack of response from him wasn't what I had expected. Not that anything he said would change the fact that I have been taking action where he has failed.

The path opened to a sight that made us both pause. Among the stark mountain rocks bloomed an impossible garden, one that rivaled my grandmother's. Roses climbed trellises, herbs spilled from beds, fruit trees were heavy with ripe offerings. Vibrant flowers littered the grass around us. A cottage sat in the middle, smoke curling from its chimney. As we approached the door, I could make out a soft shuffling from inside.

"Welcome, children." A voice like honey and thorns drifted from inside. "Please, do come in."

I exchanged a wary glance with Kyler before pushing open the wooden door.

CHAPTER 7

The cottage door creaked open to reveal a plump woman with silvery hair piled atop her head. Ancient eyes pierced through me from her weathered face. I fought the urge to step back, to retreat from that milky gaze that, though unseeing, seemed all-knowing.

My skin crawled as she circled us, her tattered dress trailing dead leaves across the wooden floor. "Death's pretty pet comes at last to claim her fate," she cackled, her voice like honey dripping over broken glass. The sound raised gooseflesh along my arms, and I clenched my fists to steady myself.

Kyler shifted closer to me, his shoulder brushing mine—a silent and surprising reminder I wasn't facing this alone. The warmth of him was an anchor in this unsettling place. Dried herbs hung from the ceiling beams, filling the air with an earthy sweetness that couldn't quite mask the underlying scent of decay. Bones clattered somewhere in the shadows as she moved, tiny skeletal fingers tapping against jars of unidentifiable contents. They were nothing I've ever seen compared to my grandmother's medical stores.

I squared my shoulders, refusing to be this woman's prey. My heart thundered, but I wouldn't show fear. "I've come to learn how I may change my fate," I said, proud that my voice didn't waver despite the dread pooling in my stomach.

"Sit, sit, the tea grows cold." She gestured to a small table where cups appeared, filled with a dark liquid that hadn't been there moments before. As I took my seat, I peered into the delicate porcelain, but my reflection rippled wrong on the surface, distorting into shapes I couldn't comprehend—faces that weren't mine staring back with hollow eyes. "You may call me Elisanna."

"My name's Alora. I hope you don't mind that we came to see you."

"I know exactly who you are, child. Fate is ever changing, my dear, yet never changes at all," she intoned, her fingers dancing over the rim of her cup. "It's quite maddening when you think about it." She erupted in a fit of cackles.

My hands fisted under the table, ready to upturn it and bolt out the door at a moment's notice. I sensed warmth to my left as Kyler covered my hand with his larger one. Though his shoulders were tight, he didn't seem fazed by the witch.

"What do you mean? How can something change and not?" I asked.

"It is as I say," she took a sip of her tea, a dark bead of liquid running from the corner of her mouth. "Fate is like water. It can feel cool on a summer day, burn so hot the skin melts off your bones, or harden with a deep freeze. Yet, once that boiling cools, or the ice melts, it's returned to the same state. It's true form." I tried not to look so taken aback by her sudden lucidity as she turned towards Kyler. "It's been a while since I've seen you. You were just a princeling. Messing about in an old crone's garden. It seems you've also come wanting something from me, yet again."

Kyler shifted in his seat, his shoulders squared back as if he was preparing to face a beast. "I—"

"I already know what it is you want." She spat. "And you know you're a fool to think it. You'd do well to appreciate the gift you've been given, even if you believe there is a mistake. Fate makes no mistakes." A loud cackle emitted from her once again before she quiets just for a moment. Eyes fixed on the empty space beyond us, the silence broken by a sudden muttering tangent of nonsense.

My head spun, trying to follow her words, each phrase like a puzzle piece that refused to connect. She grabbed my wrist with surprising strength, her fingers cold as grave dirt, and vision flashed behind my eyes - waves crashing against distant shores I'd never seen, salt spray on my lips, the cry of unfamiliar birds.

"Can't change what's written in blood, though a bond for a bond is a fickle thing." Her lucid gaze met mine, white eyes somehow focusing on me, seeing through the layers of my soul. "Fate's threads are already woven, never to be unwoven. Never to fray." The smell of citrus and rain mingled in the air before seeming to flow out to be replaced by the earthy herbs that litter the space.

Kyler tried to pull me back, his fingers closing protectively around my elbow, but she hissed at his interference like a feral cat. I felt him tense beside me. "Death walks beside you, little hunter. Runerth lies beyond the monster's maw. Isles of stone, isles of old, isles always lost. Never found. Can you be found? Are you lost? Death's pretty pet, pretty pretty pet, can never see. Always blind. Left behind. Abandoned. Trust the bound, don't be found. Life must die, so Death will rise. Dark stone drenched in blood. You'll kill the sun." My heart pounded against my ribs. I went rigid hearing the nickname Maël always called me. She continued, her voice dropping to a reverent whisper, "Worthy you'll be when the crown, the blade and the mask meet. The balance of three to right one's wrong."

Her words echoed strangely as shadows danced on the cottage walls, moving against the light in ways that defied explanation. "North wind carries truth," she laughed. "Bonds break and reform anew."

My head throbbed with each cryptic phrase, each word

burrowing into my mind like thorns. The tea cups shattered on the floor as she declared, "Time flows backward in their waters. Fate's weaver ties the strings. The strings!" Her eyes rolled back as magic crackled through the air, raising the hairs on my arms and leaving a metallic tang in my mouth from the power.

"Choose wisely which bonds to keep," she rasped. My fingers trembled against the table edge as she slumped in her chair, suddenly frail as if the prophecy had drained her life force. Blood dripped from her nose in a thin crimson line as she whispered, "The harbinger of flame will cleanse this land, will save us all." The words settled over me like a shroud, a promise and a threat intertwined.

CHAPTER 8

Her cryptic words haunted us as we left the witch's dusty home, each step down the mountain taking us further from her cottage, but not from the burden of her prophecy. My hands wouldn't stop shaking despite the warm afternoon sun beating down on us, my fingers trembling like autumn leaves in a storm. The twisted words clung to my thoughts, an unwelcome shadow I couldn't shake off.

Kyler walked ahead, his shoulders rigid with tension. The phrase "a bond for a bond" kept repeating in my thoughts like a haunting melody I couldn't shake, like a curse whispered directly into my soul.

The mountain path seemed twice as steep going down, or maybe it was just the heaviness in my chest making each step harder. I felt mildly relieved when the makeshift campsite came into view. Without a word, I began fretting over the horses, brushing my hand over their smooth coats, calming the doubts that have now taken residence in my mind. I caught Rasher casting concerned glances my way, but I couldn't meet his eyes, afraid he'd see the fear that had taken root inside me.

Fate's threads were already woven. The words twisted in my gut like a knife. What did that mean for my future, for all our futures? Were we merely puppets dancing on strings I couldn't see? Cheap entertainment for the gods above.

I felt as if something vital had been removed from my chest, leaving only questions and dread. This meeting with a loon of a woman had carved a void where certainty once lived. Oryn and I were forever linked, a bond that nothing could break. I cursed Fate for such a cruel hand. Forced to love the man who left me to rot in a cell, all for a power he coveted that I'm not too sure he didn't receive thanks to the Alchemist.

"Are you satisfied now?" Kyler finally broke the oppressive silence among us, his deep voice startling me from my spiral of thoughts.

"Clearly, this isn't the face of satisfaction, or have you never satisfied a woman?" I snapped, the words coming out sharper than I'd intended, brittle as thin ice. His jaw tightened as he turned away again, adding another layer to the tension between us. Another bridge burned by my quick tongue.

The weight of destiny sat heavy on my shoulders, a burden I never asked for. I couldn't outrun fate—the very thought made me want to scream into the endless sky above us, to tear at the fabric of reality until it unraveled.

Under his breath, Kyler mumbled something about stubborn fae women before angrily leaving. I pretended not to hear him, my fingers brushing against the dagger at my side for comfort, wishing for the familiar feeling of the one I left behind to ground me. Our trip down the mountain was now blanketed with a welcomed silence.

As dusk settled over the forest, we made camp. The fire crackled between us, an uncrossable barrier of flames and unspoken words. The dancing shadows seemed to mock me, reminding me of Elisanna's blind eyes that somehow saw too much.

"Want to talk about it?" Rasher asked gently, his voice carrying across the campfire, laced with genuine concern.

I shook my head, the words stuck in my throat. Above us, stars wheeled across the vast darkness, but sleep refused to come. I traced constellations until my eyes burned, searching for answers in their ancient patterns, hoping they might reveal some secret the witch had kept hidden. Something that would help me break free of Oryn. The woman's twisted cackling haunting my mind as I finally succumbed to my exhaustion.

Dawn brought no clarity. The rising sun painted the world in soft gold, but my mind remained clouded with questions. As I rolled up my bedroll, I felt Kyler's gaze following my movements, his eyes heavy with unasked questions. Probably wondering how my bloodlust hasn't caused me to stab him in his sleep. He might not be entirely wrong about my nature, since I considered it several times, but luckily for him he has done nothing unforgivably wrong yet, but with nobles it's always a matter of time.

"We need to work together." His words came out stiff and formal, like he was addressing a stranger rather than the woman he's spent the last few days with, someone he didn't deem worthy of saving.

"Now you believe the murderer's skills are valuable to you?" The accusation tasted bitter on my tongue, poisonous and unfair. His face darkened like a thundercloud, jaw clenched tight enough I could see the muscle jump beneath his skin. I wasn't even sure what we'd work together on...it was clear we would never see eye to eye and he saw me as a hinderance. We'd return to the castle, I'd meet with the queen, and hopefully be sent on my merry way to figure out how to fix my mess of a life.

It didn't take long for us to pack up and continue down to the town we stopped in prior. The feeling of dancing with Kyler ghosting across my skin like a favored song now lost to time.

Our horses trotted side by side as we continued down the path back to the cove, the sound a lulling rhythm that kept us pacing along. Tears burned behind my eyes, frustrated that the witch didn't relay what I had hoped. But I couldn't let this disappointment take over. I still had Johan to kill, figuring out a way to deal with Ryn would come next.

As the quaint little town came into view, a messenger rushed towards us, spurring his steed at a breakneck speed.

"Souoak is under siege!"

Kyler and Rasher exchanged a look. The color drained from their faces. Rasher's eyes met mine and I gave a wordless nod.

"We need to get there now," Kyler commanded, his voice ringing with authority that I couldn't help responding to. His presence was more so of a prince than what I've witnessed since meeting him.

We raced south, the wind carrying prayers I feared would go unanswered, my heart pounding with a terrible certainty that this was just the beginning of what fate had in store for us all.

CHAPTER 9

Smoke burned my lungs as I raced through Souoak's streets, the familiar paths now a maze of destruction. Despite the breakneck speed we travelled, it took days for us to reach the town in need. Once we had arrived, I ditched my horse in the coverage of the trees and marched into the fray. Kyler and Rasher looked to me as they led the way, then at each other, silent words understood between the two of them.

"Stay with us," Kyler ordered, going ahead without waiting for a response.

"I think I'll take my chances," I told Rasher before stalking away.

"Alora!" He called, but the sound of blades meeting replaced anything further. A glance back showed Rasher was clearly dominating the soldier. He buried his blade just below that gold plated chest plate and I took that as a good sign as any, it was fine to leave him.

I beckoned my shadows. Covered in inky tendrils, I was a nightmare come to life. The thrum of the battle around me urged me on. This town was all too familiar, the square, the blacksmith... the last time I traveled through, I had chased away the same people who terrorized them now. Guilt curled around my chest. I should've done more for them while I had been here. The blacksmith's forge was empty, things tossed around, blood splattered everywhere. Someone died from whatever transpired here. I prayed to the lost gods the man and his daughter made it out, though a part of me knew the blacksmith was likely fighting for his people.

I picked around the mess, looking for something more useful, when a familiar glint caught my eye on the shelf behind the counter. A single obsidian blade sat, an outlier to the set I acquired years ago. I snatched it, thankful for how well the hilt fit my palm. A comfort that spurred me into action as I rushed back outside.

An elderly couple cowered against a building, the old man pushing the woman behind him, trying to hold back their attacker with nothing more than a wooden staff. The soldier didn't notice me behind him until I gripped his cold iron shoulder and brought my other arm in front of him, dragging a dagger along his exposed neck. It didn't surprise me how easy it was to steel my mind to nothing but the fight around us.

Souoakians ran from all directions, trying to avoid the blades raining down upon them. Sunneva's wave of brutes overrode the town. Smoke tainted the air as entire buildings succumbed to flames. The screams of women and children permeating the air. Johan be damned. I'll eventually catch up to that slimy bastard one day, but Sunneva needed to be stopped. Kyler can criticize my profession all he wants, but bringing this war to innocents for personal gain is beyond acceptable.

This was one of the genuine horrors of the world. Mindless slaughter to elevate status. How could Oryn bear this burden? I shook my head. Why did I ever believe I knew him? He played me, enraptured me with pretty words, every touch more addicting than the last, all pieces to his game. A game I was sure I wouldn't lose again.

Innocent people fell around me, no matter how many soldiers I slaughtered. Every life lost today I'd be sure to pay back the golden prince in kind. He would feel the pain hundreds have endured thanks to the southern empire he was due to inherit.

Blood dripped from my blade, leaving a crimson trail in my wake. Each swing sent fire through my muscles, but every strike found its mark—another Sunnevean soldier falling to me.

Their bodies littered the cobblestones, gilded uniforms I once saw everywhere now stained with death. A child's scream cut through the clash of steel, stopping me mid-stride. Two tiny figures huddled in a doorway, their eyes wide with terror, clutching each other as if that alone might shield them from the horrors around us.

"This way," I called, banishing my shadows to give them a reassuring smile as I extended my hand to them. The thunder of armored footsteps echoed behind us—knights in pursuit. My heart dropped as we rounded a corner. Wrong turn. The alley ended in a solid wall, the stone face mocking my terrible sense of direction at the worst of times.

"Stay behind me," I pushed the children back, positioning myself between them and danger. Two knights blocked our escape, their armor gleaming in the firelight, reflecting the burning buildings around us. The children coughed behind me. I needed to get them out of here fast before their lungs took in too much of the thick smoke. Pain lanced through my heart as I tried to stay upright through its wave. How much longer could I go on if this blasted bond continued to threaten me?

The soldiers advanced and steel rang against steel as I parried the first strike, the impact jarring up my arm. My blade found the gap between chest plate and shoulder. I buried it to the hilt until the cry building in his throat silenced before it rang out. Pain exploded in my side as the second knight's sword caught me. Blood seeped through my leathers, hot and sticky, each breath becoming a battle of its own.

The knight froze, his eyes widening beneath his helm.

"Lady Alora? The prince has been—"

My dagger slid between his ribs, cutting off whatever false narrative the crown has been spewing. The thought of every Sunnevean here has seen my face, ready to drag me back to that hell for a handsome reward made my skin crawl. But I couldn't let that deter me now, fighting for every breath and trying to stand to my full height. I would not die in front of these poor children. I would not add to their trauma and I will see them to safety.

My feet stumbled with every step, mere feet feeling like miles as we moved away from the alley. The onslaught calming, my vision was spotty but there were less gaudy gold uniforms than there had been when I arrived. I urged the tiny humans on, focusing on one leaden step at a time. If we could just reach the trees, they'd have a chance. I focused with each strained breath on finding a spot near where, hopefully, my horse remained, to avoid being stranded. Rasher was far too large to ride with, and Kyler was far too cantankerous. Worst case, I'd steal Rasher's before having to ride with the prince.

"Run," I gasped to the children, pressing a hand to my wound. "Hide until it's quiet. Find somewhere they won't be able to see you." They looked hesitant, but after another prompt to hurry, they disappeared into the shadows, their tiny feet barely making a sound.

My vision blurred as I slumped against a wall, the sounds of battle growing distant. Time slipped away like water through my fingers until footsteps approached—different from before, but familiar. They were lighter, and more purposeful, the stride of someone who knew exactly where they were going. Life must be so much easier when you knew where your path led.

"Well, this seems familiar," Kyler's voice cut through the haze, his sarcastic tone somehow comforting now.

Strong arms lifted me from the blood-stained ground. The gash at my side burned at the movement, but my heart found reprieve in his arms, though that may be because I was fading fast.

"You shouldn't have run off," he muttered, his breath warm against my ear as he held me tight against his chest. "You're the bane of my existence, you know that?"

The world spun as he carried me. "The children—" I whispered, my fingers weakly clutching at his shirt.

"Safe," he promised. "We found them while looking for you. They're with the other survivors." His voice softened just enough that I wondered if I'd imagined it.

Darkness crept at the edges of my sight, but I felt his heart beating steady against my cheek, a rhythm to focus on as pain threatened to pull me under.

"Stay awake, Princess."

The nickname caught me off guard—so different from his usual cold, dismissive tone. I must be dying for him to grace me with such kindness. Something in the way he said it made my heart stutter. Maybe that was just the blood loss talking.

CHAPTER 10

My eyes fluttered open to unfamiliar wooden beams crossing the ceiling, their dark wood a stark contrast to the pale morning light. Soft sheets cradled my aching body, every breath sending ripples of pain through my side. The scent of herbs and pine hung in the air—unfamiliar yet somehow comforting.

Kyler sat in a chair beside the bed, his eyes distant as he stared out the window. From this angle, he looked more... real. Gone was the celebrated swordsman I met as my estranged husband's best friend, but so was the righteous prince quick to pass judgement. The shadows under his eyes spoke of sleepless nights, though it failed to dim his handsome face. His fingers absently traced patterns on the armrest, a nervous habit I hadn't noticed before.

"How long was I out?" My voice cracked, dry and rough like I'd swallowed sand.

"Four days." He didn't look at me, just continued staring at whatever held his attention beyond the glass.

Silence stretched between us like a physical thing, heavy with unspoken words. The crackle of the hearth fire filled the space between us. I shifted, wincing as pain lanced through my ribs.

"I saw what you did out there," he spoke first, his voice low, almost reverent. "Thank you for helping them. I'll forever be in your debt."

The memory of blood and steel flashed behind my eyes—the children's terror, the knights, the spray of crimson that seemed to follow me. My hands moved with deadly precision, a practiced dance, now pure instinct.

"Just don't arrest me for murdering Sunneva's soldiers whenever you go back to being Oryn's right-hand man." Bitterness coated my words like poison. The name tasted like ash on my tongue.

Kyler's jaw tightened at the mention of his friend, a muscle jumping beneath his skin. His fingers stilled on the armrest, knuckles whitening.

"The thought never crossed my mind," he sighed, one hand moving to his temple. His arm dropped once again as his eyes lifted to the ceiling. A forced resolve shattered the mask he usually hid behind.

"Tell me about it," he whispered, an invitation rather than a demand. For once, there was no hatred laced in his words, no wall between us. Leaning over to the table beside the bed, he brought a cup of water to my lips. I grabbed the cup, my fingers brushing his, our eyes meeting before he relinquished it. Cool water eased the burning of my throat. "I swear you can trust me. I just want to understand."

Pain, old and deep, unfurled in my chest. Words spilled out like water from a broken dam and I didn't know how to stop myself. The village burning under Johan's hand, Oryn's false promises and the betrayal that cut deeper than any blade. I told him things I'd never spoken aloud, memories I'd locked away so tightly they'd nearly suffocated me. Things like losing Maël, how it felt to be mated without knowing and forced to love someone.

The Alchemist's words echoed in my mind, their cruel laughter mixing with the screams of the dying. "Such potential wasted on you," they had purred, those glittering markings on their skin catching the firelight as the blood in my veins burned from his injections.

"He knew," my voice broke, tears burning behind my eyes. "He knew and left me there." The admission felt like ripping an old wound, fresh blood spilling forth.

Kyler's fingers curled into fists, knuckles white with rage. Something dangerous flickered in his eyes—a cold fury that reminded me of winter storms. Even the air seemed to bite like the first day of winter.

"Nothing can be done. The witch confirmed that much with her riddles." I whispered into the quiet. Elisanna's nonsensical words that once plagued my mind with confusion, no, *haunted* me with their clarity.

His eyes finally met mine, something vulnerable lurking in their depths. The hardened warrior momentarily fractured, revealing glimpses of the man beneath.

"Sometimes fate is cruel," he said. A bitter laugh escaped him. "I wanted to ask the witch about something similar in nature. But as you heard, she was quick to dismiss me before I could ask."

"What did you want to ask?"

He scratched at his jaw, a moment of hesitation. "I found my mate recently, but I wanted to see if it could be ignored. If one could refuse the bond and live without repercussions."

My heart stuttered at his words, a strange hollowness opening in my chest. "You'd choose not to seal your bond?"

"She'd never choose me. I'd never force myself upon her, no matter how captivating I found her."

Sleep tugged at my consciousness, the pain dragging me under. The edges of my vision darkened, his face becoming a blur.

"That's silly," I mumbled, fighting to keep my eyes open. "Any woman would be lucky..." The words slurred on my tongue, refusing to form. "You're..."

"You've been through enough..." his softened voice barely registered in my ears. Was I already dreaming, conjuring up kind words just because he gave me space to tell my tale? What was it called when you grew fond of an enemy? Was he even my enemy? My thoughts floated in a million different directions as darkness pulled me into oblivion once again.

CHAPTER 11

I woke to sunlight streaming through the window, the pain in my side reduced to a dull ache. Thankfully, no guests this time, at least until Rasher came in to check on me and fill me in on Souoak. Five days had passed since the battle, but we had been able to turn the tide. Kyler sent reinforcements to protect the town while they focused on rebuilding. There were far too many casualties, but many lived. Many who would've died otherwise. My wounds finally healed enough that I could move without wincing. Not completely. The scar ached with every stretch, but it was enough. Rasher left the tiny room I was occupying so I could bathe and get dressed. Someone left a simple shirt and leather pants for me; my pretty boots looked aged but still intact. The obsidian dagger I pilfered from the blacksmith's shop lay on the table beside the bed. I slid it into my boot before striding out of the room.

Stairs creaked below each step as I descended, realizing they had me in a small inn as the bar opened up below. Rasher's eyes tracked me until I sat beside him, passing over a roll and some meat. I didn't realize how hungry I had been until my stomach growled. I bit into the savory bread, holding back a moan of delight.

Kyler watched me with intensity, a frown tugging at his lips before going back to whatever they had been discussing prior to my arrival. From the sound of it, they were making plans to send resources and move troops.

"I need to go to Bridgedale," I told Kyler. "Vanya will have more information on what's happening, and it's your best shot at protecting your people from another skirmish."

His eyes narrowed. "You're not fully recovered."

"I'm recovered enough." I waved my hand. "Unless you plan to tie me to a bed until you deem me well and truly healed, I'm going."

Something flashed in his eyes before he looked away. "We'll leave at dusk."

"You don't need to go with me. There are things that need your attention here."

Kyler's eyes met mine, his mouth formed into a tight line. "Rasher and I have spent the last few days making arrangements while you slept. Believe it or not, I have things in order. We've got a few loose ends to tie up and then we'll head out."

Caught in a stalemate with Kyler's hard stare, Rasher snickered to my left, glad he thought this was amusing.

"Fine, but may I make one suggestion?" I asked.

"What's that?"

"Let me do the talking. Wouldn't want you to upset the wrong person and end up at the end of their blade."

Rasher's snickers erupted into laughter as he shook his head. A cocky smile spread across my face, waiting for the fallout. Disappointment filled me when it never came. Instead, Kyler flashed me a heart-stopping grin.

"As you wish, Princess."

We slipped into Bridgedale under the cover of darkness, hoods pulled low over our faces. The familiar streets welcomed me like an old friend, though tension hung in the air. War had changed even this place. As we stalked the streets, posters of my face with words like "kidnapped" and "missing" littered every wall and window alongside conscription notices. Sunneva was continuing to build its army. Another battle was surely on the horizon.

The familiar scent of leather and steel filled Vanya's guild hall as we entered through the back entrance. Assassins milled about, more than usual, preparing for what looked like some kind of celebration. Black banners draped the stone walls, and the sound of laughter echoed off the high ceiling.

"Remember, not a word." I reminded my companions as I guided them through the crowd with my head held high.

Music pulsed through the crowded hall, the beat matching the thrum of my heart. Everywhere I looked, faces were alight with drunken merriment already.

Vanya's feline grin appeared through the crowd, her eyes widening when they landed on me.

"The prodigal daughter returns," she called, cutting through the throng with predatory grace.

She pulled me into a tight embrace, the scent of jasmine and blade oil clinging to her skin. "Perfect timing. We're celebrating."

Around us, assassins raised glasses, toasting with one another. Kyler accepted a drink from a passing server, his posture loosening.

"What's happening?" I asked.

"Depends on who you ask," Vanya said cryptically, pressing a glass of wine into my hand. "You know, it doesn't take much for any of these men to drink." She gestured around at the guild members.

"Alora!" A shout echoed from my right before I'm accosted by muscular arms, bright blond hair flashing in my vision as I'm lifted and spun around in the air. "I knew you'd make it to my birthday!" Lucas set me down before pulling me into a strong hug. Over his shoulder, Kyler's eyes appeared to narrow at my friend's close proximity. Of course, he was grumpy once again. He was in a room surrounded by criminals. Just because we've reached some semblance of peace didn't mean everyone else got as much grace.

Lucas finally noticed Rasher and Kyler. He took them in with an appreciative glance, taking his sweet time on Rasher, who didn't appear ready to condemn him. "And you've brought quite the gift."

Kyler growled as I stepped in between him and Lucas. "They're my...." I struggled to find the words. Rasher was a new friend, but Kyler... "companions. I'll make up your gift to you another day. I promise to make it extra special."

Lucas pouted before patting my shoulder. "I'm just glad to see you alive, Lor. People are saying you were kidnapped. No one's seen you since your wedding."

"We'll talk about it tomorrow," I hooked my arm in his, pulling him towards the reverie and gesturing for Kyler and Rasher to follow. "Let's see how much you can drink, birthday boy."

"Like a fish," Lucas smirked.

As the night progressed in a blur of music and laughter, I nursed my single glass of wine, watching Kyler from across the room. His shoulders had relaxed for the first time in days, his cheeks flushed with each new toast. His smile came easier now, it even reached his eyes. I was surprised to see him enjoying himself. Lucas and Rasher danced as the music heightened, the scene almost becoming overwhelming.

"You're a rowdy bunch," Kyler mused. "Especially your master," he pointed towards Vanya, who was dancing on a far table while pouring more drinks.

"Yeah," I smiled, "it's easy to accept such a gift when you know how fleeting life is." His shoulder brushed my own as I became aware of how close he was. "I hope we didn't disappoint your expectations. You know, being cold-blooded killers and all."

He choked on his drink, spewing the deep red liquid down his shirt. Seeing the prince in so much disarray was oddly satisfying.

"Let's get you cleaned up." With a laugh, I motioned him to follow me. Once we were out of the dining hall, I could hear the even thud of his steps behind me as we ascended the stairs. The manor hadn't changed at all since I left. I led him down the hall until we came upon my room, the heavy oak door creaking open as I stepped across the threshold.

Kyler stopped before entering, looking unsure if he should come into my space.

"It's okay," I said. "I have an extra shirt you can change into and an ensuite to clean up."

With eyes cast down, he finally stepped inside, quietly shutting the door behind him. I turned to my wardrobe to pull out the shirt that was always way too large on my frame. It should fit him fine. When I turned back, he was pulling his soiled shirt over his head.

Kyler was more than just a pretty face, his body was a work of art. A broad chest with fine dark hair that trailed down his abdomen until it seemed to go further than the V at his hips, disappearing beneath his pants. Creamy skin interrupted by scars here and there only seemed to accentuate the lean muscle that years of training had sculpted. He turned his back to me to drop his weapons on my desk. I couldn't help but notice the expanse of his back and how well it too was toned.

A nervous cough brought me back to reality as he stood before me with his arms crossed and an eyebrow raised.

"Right." I could feel the heat rising to my cheeks. I thrust the shirt into his chest and pointed to the bathroom door. "You can clean up in there."

"Thanks," the corner of his mouth lifted in amusement before he sauntered into the ensuite, shutting the door quietly behind him.

I scolded myself for so obviously staring. He had only just stopped looking at me without such a hateful gaze, and now I was ogling him like a wolf to a lamb. I started to pace, looking around for anything possibly out of place since I was gone. As always, it seemed no one entered my room. A respect among the guild members.

That's when I saw it—something familiar glinting on my desk. An obsidian dagger, one that matched my set that was missing since one of my last missions with Lucas. The sight of it stopped my breath. I picked it up, inspecting it. Sure enough, it fit into my palm just as all of them did.

The sound of the door opening made me whirl, blade still in my hand.

"Where did you get this?" I asked.

"A woman I danced with dropped it." His words caused me to halt, even my breath slowing as he took a careful step towards me. "It was here in Bridgedale. I had been in town and subjected to attending the governor's ball. Hating every moment until she twirled into my arms, then she quickly disappeared into the night. This blade left in her wake."

The governor's ball... horror flowed through me, my mind trying to reconcile that night with this new information. Could it be? Kyler, the stranger I danced with, the one who chased me as I ran after our mark? It didn't make sense. Of all the fae to cross paths with, how could that man have been him? Thought after thought forced its way into the forefront of my mind, rethinking every interaction I've had with him. Did he know it was me from the very beginning? Surely not. I pushed that idea away, not after how he looked at me in Esmeray when he found out who I was. No matter how hard I tried, I couldn't make it make sense.

His voice dropped low, dark eyes never left mine. "I never thought I'd see her again. That was, until I arrived at her engagement party. Suddenly, the woman fate continued to drive me to seek was mated with one of my closest friends."

It hit like a sudden wave, crashed into all of my senses while I was too oblivious to see the warning signs. The mate he mentioned before, the one he thought would never choose him. She was me. I felt mortified that I never put it all together, of course he would've rather chosen to live without completing the bond. He went from calling me a murderer to listening to me talk about being hurt by another.

"How long have you known?"

"I suspected when Oryn introduced you, I had brushed off the weird sensation in my gut as caused by something served at your engagement party. But I knew for sure when I carried you out of the burning dungeon. The pain I felt watching you fall, the way your presence seemed to engulf me as I held you close." His dark eyes met mine, inherently sober despite the drinks he'd consumed.

My grip tightened on the blade. "And you didn't think to tell me?"

The space between us disappeared as he stepped before me. "After what you told me about Oryn and how you felt forced into the bond..." Pain flashed across his features, raw and unguarded. "You deserved a choice."

The words hit like physical blows.

"Even if it means never having my true mate," he added quietly.

His confession hung between us in the dim light. I already had a mate...how could I have another? My thoughts raced and yet the witch's cackling echoed in the distance: *a bond for a bond.*

My heart pounded against my ribs as it all clicked into place. The realization stole my voice.

CHAPTER 12

My mind whirled with Elisanna's words, pieces of it spinning like autumn leaves in a tempest. I could almost smell the sickly scent of her cottage.

"A bond for a bond." The words echoed in my skull, no longer mere riddles, but a key to salvation. My heart thundered against my ribs, each beat a desperate rhythm of possibility.

I watched Kyler through the flickering candlelight, his severe expression softened by wine, my dagger still in my hand. The air between us crackled with unspoken tension, heavy with the weight of destiny.

"You were the answer this whole time." The words slipped from my lips. My fingers trembled as I traded the weapon for my wineglass, needing something to ground me in this moment.

His brow furrowed. "The answer to what?" The low timbre of his voice sent shivers down my spine, and I watched as he leaned forward, closing the distance between us inch by torturous inch.

Elisanna's words about fate rang in my memory—not about changing it, but about forging new paths. Perhaps I could weave my own thread into destiny's tapestry. My pulse quickened as it all began to make sense, each revelation striking like lightning in my mind.

I clutched my wine glass tighter, watching Kyler's expression shift from confusion to curiosity.

"The witch, she was trying to tell me," my voice trembled with the weight of my realization. "I was hoping to change my fate, to break my bond."

Kyler's eyes narrowed. "Break your bond?"

"A bond for a bond," I whispered, the words heavy with meaning. "What if we could break my bond with Oryn?"

He stiffened. "I don't recall her mentioning breaking bonds. She was clear that what fate designed was resolute."

"Yes, but she suggested trading one bond for another. To be free of the bond with Oryn, I need a new mate bond." My eyes met his, confusion shining in them. "If we complete our bond, then I could be released from the other." The words hung between us, dangerous and electric.

Kyler's jaw clenched. "That's not something to be taken lightly."

"I know what I'm asking." I leaned forward, my heart hammering against my ribs. "You said it yourself—you'd suffer not having your true mate if it meant giving me a choice."

"And now you're choosing to use our bond as a weapon?" His voice was cold, but his eyes burned.

I flinched. "Not a weapon. Freedom."

"Freedom?" He laughed bitterly. "If you feel trapped being bound to one prince, how are you going to feel being bound to me? You'd be trading one cage for another."

"It wouldn't be like that with you," I insisted.

He stepped further into my space, so close my face was tilted up just to meet his piercing gaze. "How can you be so sure? You don't even know me, you don't even like my mere presence."

"Only when you're being insufferable." My voiced softened. "I feel like I've learned enough to know, to trust, that things would be different with you. I know what the pain of being separated from a mate feels like, and it's too great to bear for a lifetime. But when you've been near, it's lessened. You're the only one who can help me."

Kyler shook his head. "This is madness, Lor. Not only are you married, but you're the gods damned princess of the very kingdom at war with my own."

"Princess only by marriage," my correction earned me a sharp look from the imposing male. "Maybe it is madness, but it's the only path I see forward."

"And after? When Oryn's bond is broken? What then?" His question cut to the heart of my uncertainty.

I swallowed hard. "We... figure it out. Together."

"You're asking me to bind myself to you forever on the promise of 'figuring it out'?" The hurt in his voice was palpable. "It wasn't that long ago we were at each other's throats. Are you going to stop slaying anyone who crosses your path? Because that is where 'together' will lead."

I huffed. "I find that oddly ironic coming from someone who plotted a king's assassination. Rasher kills people for you. How is that any different?"

"It just is." He all but shouted. "Hundreds will fall if he's allowed to continue on."

"And yet, every time someone didn't walk away from meeting me, an insurmountable amount of lives were spared." I held onto my confidence like it was the only shield protecting me from the intensity of his stare. "I'm asking you to trust me," I whispered. "Like I'm trusting you."

His hands cupped my face, eyes searched mine for the answers he sought. "I can't do this and not fall madly in love with you. You know what will happen once this is sealed? There's no resisting it." His thumb brushed along my jawline. "Every breath that I breathe would be for you. Every thought would be of you. My very reason for being, you. I would be yours, but you would also be mine. And I just don't believe you understand how much you're asking for here."

"What can I do to gain your favor? You said you were indebted to me for saving your people. I would be indebted to you for saving me." I pleaded.

His thumb traced my lips, pressing into the plumpness of my bottom lip. "Say you want to be mine. You don't need to mean it now, but one day. Allow me to follow you until the end, when the god of death comes to collect my last breath. I will earn your heart every moment of every day if I have to. But don't dismiss the possibility of what we could be. I have no expectations of you other than not leaving my side, but that is for my own selfish desire to keep you safe."

His confession held my heart in a vice grip. Kyler was honest to a fault, baring his feelings, knowing full well I could destroy them with simple words. He was asking so little of me when it seemed like I was asking for the world. Maybe someday I could love him in earnest. I knew the bond would continue to bring us together and feed our desire. Unlike before, I'd be going into this knowing what's happening, consenting to it. After what I've seen since traveling with him, I knew the loyalty I once questioned was there. Oryn may have been able to betray me, but I knew Kyler would fight alongside me to save his people.

"I want to be yours," I whispered, the truth of it burning through my veins like wildfire.

CHAPTER 13

His lips crashed into mine, stealing my breath and thoughts in one devastating moment. The fire raced through my blood, igniting every nerve ending as our bodies pressed together, fitting perfectly as if we'd been crafted for each other.

His fingers tangled in my hair, tilting my head back to deepen the kiss, claiming me with a possession that should have frightened me but instead felt like coming home. We moved backwards until I felt my bed on the back of my knees. We separated from each other just long enough for me to pull my top over my head. Strong arms wrapped around my legs as Kyler picked me up and laid me on the bed before him. I slid my pants past my thighs and tossed them away once my legs were free. My skin felt cold with the absence of his hands as I watched him untie his strings and step out of his pants, his length fisted in his large hand. His intimidating size had my core dripping with anticipation. A whine escaped my throat as I watched him palm it while his gaze locked onto my core.

"Patience, Princess. I believe someone questioned my ability to satisfy a woman." He dropped to his knees, pulling me so my legs draped over his shoulders, my rear nearly off the edge. "This is your last chance to back out of this, Lor."

I shook my head. With every word, his breath brushed along my most sensitive area, and I was ready to beg for him.

A dark chuckle emitted from him before he slowly licked slowly up my center before his lips came down, sucking on the bundle of nerves that had my back already arching off the bed. Cries escaped me as I fisted my hand in his dark hair, pulling him closer, desperate for more friction. He continued to lick me with no abandon, pleased hums came from him as he slipped a finger, then two, into me. The feeling of fullness bringing my pleasure crashing down.

After the shockwaves of my orgasm waned, he stood up, rubbing the head of his cock in my slickness.

"You taste fucking divine," he mused, his voice low. One hand notched himself to my entrance while the other reached out to cup my breast. "You're absolute perfection." He brought his mouth down, sucking a taunt nipple into his mouth. He released it with a pop as he peppered my stomach with kisses, working his way back down until he straightened once more.

Slowly, ever so slowly, he pushed inside me. Every inch stretched me further than before and it was the most satisfying burn I've ever experienced. He kept his eyes on my face as he thrust deeper until he was fully inside me.

"Kyler," I cried as he began pumping in a steady rhythm, slowly increasing, his hands gripping my hips.

"This pussy was made for my cock, fuck I want to tie you to my bed and fuck you until you're delirious with pleasure."

I was already beginning to feel the pressure of another orgasm building, the wave climbing higher and higher and yet I wasn't at that tipping point yet.

"Who am I, Alora?" He demanded, each word coming out confident despite our panting. One of his hands reached down to circle my clit. The pressure was building and building...

"Mine." My answer came out in a breathy moan and my vision began to blacken.

"Mmm, and who are you, Princess?"

His controlled pace becomes harder, more possessive with every passing moment.

"Yours, I'm yours."

Harder and harder, his fingers continued to play with my clit while his other hand kept me planted in an angle, allowing him to brush along that sensitive spot inside me. I felt myself begin to crest over the wave as his pace grew more frantic. His name was a moan on my lips while he said mine as if it was a gift bestowed upon him. I tightened around him. My orgasm consumed him, pushing him over the edge. His cock pulsed inside me and sent me into another orgasm instantly.

His touch ignited me, each caress drawing sounds I didn't recognize from my throat, vulnerability I'd never allowed myself to show. Stars burst behind my eyes as power surged through our connections, building to something ancient and primal.

That string that led from him to me snapped open in my mind, like a door flung wide, and a flood of sensations overwhelmed me. Two distinct presences filled my thoughts, one burning bright with desire and possession, the other warm as summer and just as fierce.

Kyler's voice echoed in my head, clearly as if he'd spoken aloud, resonating through my very soul.

Mine.

But then another presence stirred—familiar yet distant and calculating. My blood ran cold as recognition dawned, the weight of it sinking into my bones like winter frost.

Oryn's voice cut through, confusion coloring his tone.

Alora...?

Horror followed quickly. *Why the fuck can I hear Kyler in your head?*

CHAPTER 14

I slammed the mental door shut, severing the connection with Oryn as panic clawed up my throat. The sensation was like shutting a physical door—jarring and final—but I knew it wouldn't hold forever. Just hearing Ryn's voice caused me to shutter. I could practically smell the grime and rot from prison... and for a moment, I was transported back to that awful place. The many tears that fell from my eyes knowing how I came to dying there.

I had been so close, so damn close to avenging my grandmother and Maël. So close to finally finding peace. All thrown away for a conniving man with a handsome smile who made me laugh. My veins cooled for a moment, panic rising in my throat remembering the feel of the serums they gave me that left me utterly weak. General torture was easy. While Vanya lived by the code of never getting caught, I could withstand a beating. But what transpired in Sunneva... the mystery serums that could block one's magic, every poke and prod, being thrown back into a cold dark cell with nothing more than stale water and moldy bread, it fed into a psychological torture that even the toughest would eventually succumb to. I could not go back, would not. I would have to steel my mind to keep the connection with him locked.

"Come back to me," Kyler whispered in my ear, saving me from my spiraling thoughts.

"I'm sorry. I didn't think my connection with him would open."

"Well," he propped up on one arm, "it was unlike anything I've felt before. I thought I was going crazy every time my legs kept bringing me to you, but now I feel that pull, almost in a physical sense. I didn't realize..."

"That you'd take up residence in my head?" I said.

"I didn't know I was speaking to you in that way. All I could think about was you."

That you're mine, Kyler sent through the bond.

I laid beside Kyler, taking him in this new light. Only days ago, we were enemies. Would this bond be enough to make this truce last? I wasn't sure I could ever give him what he wanted, especially after what happened before... but after seeing him spur into action for his people, charging into a fray of fire and death, I knew my assumption that he was a traitor was wrong. There was more beneath the surface. I just wasn't entirely sure what.

I didn't realize I had thought that out loud until Kyler tensed beside me.

"My life has been balancing on the edge of a blade, trying to bring an end to the tyrannical king." He threaded his fingers in my hair as his eyes searched my face. Heat from his body pressed against mine grounded the emotions my former lover's voice brought. "You've brought something else, something new."

"You mean Fate dragged you and tied you to your enemy?"

"Enemy," he laughed, "more like prey. I was close to finding you and I'm glad I hadn't then. Despite living a double life, I still upheld the law to some degree." His hand rested on my navel. "No, fate may have continued to push us together, but in our short time you've helped me see I haven't been doing enough. I thought I was every time I would send a warning before an attack, but there were still many casualties."

I brushed the side of his cheek, tracing down to his strong jawline. "We do what we can. There were many missions Lucas and I went on where we came back feeling defeated. Like we didn't do enough. Not doing enough doesn't equate to doing nothing. I'm sorry for insinuating as much."

"I apologize for calling you a murderer."

The word sent more knots to my stomach. As much as I liked to deflect with killing for the greater good, deep down, I still felt an immense amount of guilt for every life I took. Thankfully, the gods were long gone. The penance I would pay when Death would one day take me would be higher than I could ever afford. Nothing would await me other than a spot in fiery hell.

A strong hand gripped my chin, bringing my face up to his, brown eyes staring intently at my own. Kyler's dark eyebrows furrowed and his mouth flattened into a hard line.

"Whatever thoughts are in your head, banish them. I'd rather have you screaming at me than to see the look you had just now."

He took my mouth, his soft lips claiming mine, my hands tangled in his dark hair. More guilt clawed at me as I pushed him away.

"Please, give me some time. I don't want to lose myself in this again and end up hurt."

"You have as much as you need. I would never, ever allow any harm to come to you. I'll be here, whether you refer to me as friend or lover, or just need a punching bag."

For someone that was such a bastard the last week, he at least knew how to grovel. I sat up, the soft sheets fell around my hips as I looked at our clothes strewn across my room.

"We need to go find our friends. I'll need to talk to Vanya, too."

Kyler groaned as he watched me climb out of bed and begin grabbing fresh clothing out of the armoire.

"If we don't, they'll come looking for us...at least, Lucas will. I'm not sure I would be able to handle him making comments on your body."

Heavy footsteps thudded behind me, strong arms wrapped around my middle as Kyler pressed a gentle kiss on top of my head and took the clothing from my hands and closed the wardrobe.

"I'm sure he will leave you be for a night. Besides, he's the life of the party downstairs, surely that'll distract him enough."

I turned to find him locking my bedroom door. A small giggle left my mouth. Hopefully Lucas wouldn't barge in like the many times he had before. Something told me Kyler wouldn't take too well with another man seeing me naked. As calm and collected as he was, Kyler had ensured I knew I belonged to him now, my body was a temple for him to worship. The possessiveness surprised me as much as it thrilled me. Surely, Lucas was distracted enough to not come looking for us. Or maybe he would be too busy getting into some fun of his own to think about our absence.

"Let's return to bed, Princess." A command, not a request.

CHAPTER 15

The following morning, light streamed through the guild hall windows, painting golden stripes across the worn wooden tables. That sinking feeling returned once again. Oryn sounded relieved when he said my name. Not what I would've expected from someone who allowed some maniac to imprison his wife and experiment on her. It didn't match the dark tone he had when he had heard Kyler. And if they could hear each other in my head, did that mean they could speak amongst themselves?

As we took the carpeted steps, I gave a sideways glance at the man beside me. Kyler said he wouldn't harm me, but repeatedly said he didn't think Oryn was capable of what he did, a testament of their close friendship. As much as I wanted to fully trust him, I needed to watch my back. At any point, he might alert Oryn to our whereabouts.

Lucas waved us over to a far table laden with breakfast, his cheerful demeanor at odds with the storm brewing inside me. Rasher was already digging into a plate piled high with food. He stopped mid-bite as Kyler took a seat beside me, across from him.

"I'm surprised." Rasher said. Lucas looked up at him, just as confused as I was. "You two usually aren't so... quiet."

"It sounds like you want me to stab him. Here, I thought you were loyal to your prince."

Kyler chuckled under his breath as he added eggs and meat to his plate. He dropped some onto mine as well, which made Rasher's eyebrow raise.

"Ooooh," Lucas winked at me before nudging Rasher. "It seems they've worked out their differences."

"We did. Not that it's any of your business," Kyler's tone is clipped as he regarded Lucas, who was brimming with excitement. The moment he gets me alone, he's going to have a million questions. Many will likely have something to do with Kyler's cock.

"I'm not sure how much stake we should give the witch's words," I said. I've tried and failed at stabbing the same piece of sausage enough that I resign to picking at other items. "We need to get to Runerth, wherever that is. She said something about an island and it sounded like that was where I can untangle myself from Oryn once and for all."

"Isles," Kyler corrected. "Given her rambling sounded like a lot of nonsense, I think it would be better to try to find some old maps to locate it."

Rasher scratched his beard thoughtfully. "It's been a long time, but at one point there was an old tale of islands to the west."

Lucas perked up, leaning forward with sudden interest. "A sea voyage? Count me in."

"Who said you would be joining us?" Kyler growled, stabbing hard at his plate.

"We don't even know if they exist." I pointed out. "Lucas is coming. We need him."

"We don't need him. Rasher and I are enough." Kyler dismissed.

"If I don't go, Alora doesn't go," Lucas said. His eyes trained on Kyler, challenging him. The prince looked down at me and I gave him a shrug. "Like I would let her be near that male, prince or not, after what he did to her."

"We could put him to use." Rasher muttered, always the peace keeper.

"Thanks, big guy."

Rasher looked down to his plate once more, his cheeks slightly more pink than they had been moments ago.

I patted Kyler's arm reassuringly. "Believe it or not, he's the best thief on the continent. It's a useful skill."

"Fantastic." He deadpanned.

What is your problem? I sent to Kyler through the bond as Rasher and Lucas had begun talking about weapons and techniques.

He was all over you last night the minute he laid eyes on you.

You are being childish. It's not like that with him.

You're telling me he has never wanted to fuck you?

The air crackled with tension as I met his cold gaze, unsure of how to calm him.

Nothing has ever or will ever happen. I have enough males as it is. I winced with instant regret at the comment. *You can't let his humor rile you up, it'll only encourage him.*

Footsteps echoed across stone floors, drawing our attention. A messenger appeared at the entrance to the dining hall, scanning faces until he spotted us.

"Vanya wants you. All of you. Now."

CHAPTER 16

We filed into her office, tension following us like a ghost. The familiar space felt smaller with all of us crowded inside.

Lucas wasted no time in taking one of the chairs by the desk. He propped his boots on the solid wood surface with his usual irreverent grin, stretching back in his seat.

"What did I say about those boots?" Vanya's eyes narrowed dangerously, one finger tapping the polished surface.

Lucas grinned wider, but dropped his feet to the floor with a thud. "Just making myself comfortable."

"I'd rather you feel severely uncomfortable while you're in my office, Lucas. In fact, let's go with that moving forward." She chided before turning to me.

"Johan's been spotted in Saints Landing," Vanya announced without preamble.

I went still. Even the very breath in my lungs seemed to halt. My fingers dug into the arms of my seat, the pain of my nails biting into the hard surface helping me stay focused.

"And you trust this information?"

"I wouldn't have brought it to you if I didn't. You've held up your end of our arrangement and I would very much like for you to continue." Vanya's smile turned almost endearing. "Consider my end fulfilled."

A strong hand squeezed my shoulder. I looked up to find Kyler's gaze on me. A slight nod to Rasher from him seemed to have conveyed the importance of this.

"We can make it there within a week," Kyler stood tall, already stepping into strategy. "If we move fast—"

Lucas cut in, "What about the island and the uh," he waved his hand in the air. "The crazy, fate, rejection stuff?"

"I can arrange for a ship," Rasher added. "Maybe a half decent crew."

Lucas snorted. "And just how do we get prince charming to come? No fae would willingly break their bond."

I met Kyler's gaze once more, a silent understanding passing between us.

"He doesn't have to be willing," I said carefully.

Kyler's jaw tightened, but no disapproving comment left his mouth. It seemed he quickly realized not everything is black and white. The grey area was vast and wide.

"This plan is getting better and better!" Lucas jumped to his feet with excitement.

I brushed along the thread connecting me to Kyler. *Can we afford an extra task on top of everything else? We need to stop—*

Johan will be easy. My mate and her... friend happen to be experts in the ways of ridding someone of this world. Kyler's chuckle echoed in my head. *This man brought you a great deal of pain and shouldn't be allowed to cause anymore. Plus, you told me he works for the king. To me, it seems like we're taking a piece off the board for him. That would only benefit us.*

"We leave in two hours, Rasher, help Lucas with supplies," Kyler barked, earning him a sneer from my partner and silent acceptance from the towering man.

Kyler and I followed them out of the office but separated to my room. I sat on my plush bed and took a deep breath, steeling myself before opening the bond that connected me to Oryn. I had barely opened it when his presence flooded in, warm and desperate.

There you are, Love. Are you safe? Where—

I'm fine Oryn, but I need you to meet me at the inn in Saints Landing, I interrupted, keeping my voice steady. The sound of his voice caused a hammering in my chest, a clawing at my throat. *No guards, no attention. And I want your word that no harm will come to me.*

His sigh echoed in my mind. *I would never harm you. My heart, soul, and life are yours. I've been going mad searching for you.*

My chest tightened at his words, each one a knife twisting deeper. Lies, all lies, yet deep down I hoped he meant it, that he had some explanation.

Saints Landing, one week, I continued, pushing away any feeling other than indifference. *I also need you to pick up some items for me, that is, if my room hasn't been touched.*

I gave him instructions on finding my hidden stash in the armoire in my suite at the palace, specifically, to retrieve my knife. The last gift my grandmother had given me seemed less coincidental every time I replayed her words and the witch's in my head.

The request had been disguised innocently, a need for the only thing left of the family long departed. I was thankful he didn't ask any questions, though I'm sure they would come.

Then I snapped the bond closed with brutal force.

My body sagged forward, exhaustion washing over me. Kyler appeared in my line of sight, knelt before me, his large hands rubbed up my calves.

Guilt churned my stomach as the thought of another betrayal haunted me—not his betrayal of me, but mine of him. His words of devotion cut deeper than any blade could have and I was about to pay him back in kind ten fold.

CHAPTER 17

A week of hard riding left my thighs raw and burning. Each bounce in the saddle sent fresh pain shooting through my legs, but I kept my complaints locked behind clenched teeth. I'm sure I wasn't the only one affected by the grueling pace, but we couldn't afford to slow down.

Kyler rode beside me. At first, it wasn't so bad racing through Sunneva's grassy plains. The terrain soon turned to dry sand, so Kyler had sent tendrils of water magic behind us to smooth over our tracks. The desert drank the water faster than anything I've seen before, but it was enough to shift our trail and erase any scent we had left. It would do us no good to lead anyone directly to us.

You're doing great, Lor. It shouldn't be much longer. Kyler spoke through the bond.

This isn't my first time riding a horse, you know.

Have you gone traipsing through the desert heat for days without stopping like we have been?

My silence was met with a deep chuckle. The rumble in my mind was a welcomed distraction from the current predicament.

Thought so.

"It's just ahead," Rasher called from in front of us, his broad shoulders silhouetted against the setting sun.

A cry of excitement erupted from Lucas as he rode beside our new friend, yelling something about looking for fun. The sound of hooves battering the ground filled my ears. If it weren't for being able to talk to Kyler directly, I wouldn't have been able to understand a word from his mouth.

Salt air hit my nose as we approached Saints Landing. The briny scent grew stronger with each hoofbeat. My stomach turned, not from hunger, but from what awaited us. I've waited for this moment for years, to avenge the deaths of those I loved. I looked at my riding partner to my right. Kyler sat tall in his saddle, confident, collected. His body language gave no sign of what he was really thinking. It wasn't long ago he treated me as a criminal, deeming me nothing more than a bloodthirsty murderer. He agreed to help me because of his own heart, the one that was now bound to my own, but would that be enough to keep the peace we've finally found between us? We knew joining wasn't an act of love, at least on my part. It was survival, a means to an end. Though it made me wonder what if... what if I grew to love him? He vowed himself to me without anything in return, other than being at my side. Would he rescind that the moment I drug my knife through Johan? Killing a king who's brought nothing but war is one thing, but could his sense of justice reconcile doing so outside of the law? Not knowing what the future held riddled me with doubt.

We stabled our horses at the edge of town and continued on foot. The seaside tavern loomed ahead, its weathered sign creaking in the ocean breeze. Inside, the place reeked of fish and stale ale, the floorboards sticky with spilled drinks and who knew what else.

My eyes scanned the crowed room, passing over hardened faced until—

"There," I nodded towards Johan's blonde head at the bar. He sat hunched over a glass, oblivious to our arrival.

My hands shook as I gripped my dagger beneath my cloak. The memory of his boot on my throat, his sneering face as he commanded the village be razed, threatened to overwhelm me.

"Remember the plan," Kyler whispered, his breath warm against my ear. "Get him outside. No bloodshed in here."

I adjusted my hood, making sure my face remained hidden. One glimpse of my violet eyes would send him running and ruin everything.

Rasher positioned himself by the door, casual but alert. His massive frame blocked the exit, ready to intercept if things went wrong.

My boots stuck to the grimy floor with each step as I approached the bar. The sound of drunken laughter and clinking glasses masked my approach.

I slid onto the stool beside Johan, keeping my face angled away. His eyes immediately raked over me, lingering on the curve of my hip visible beneath my cloak.

"Buy a girl a drink?" I leaned close, disguising my voice with a higher pitch than normal.

Johan's breath stank of whiskey as he grinned, revealing teeth stained from years of drinking. "Haven't seen you here before, pretty thing."

My skin crawled at his voice, the same one that had taunted me in my darkest moments. I fought the urge to drive my dagger into his throat right there.

"Just passing through," I hummed, hating myself for the act. "Looking for a bit of... entertainment before I continue on with my journey."

He ordered another round, sliding a glass toward me with greedy eyes. I pretended to sip, letting the liquid wet my lips without swallowing. A trick Lucas had been happy to teach me when we first started working together. He kept trying to see my face, but my hood remained in place.

Four drinks later, Johan's words slurred at the edges. Perfect.

"Fresh air?" I suggested, trailing my fingers along his arm.

He slowly nodded as he slid out of his seat. He was still nimble enough not to face plant on the wooden floor, but we'd fix that shortly.

He followed me like a starved dog, stumbling slightly as we made our way toward the back door. The alley darkness swallowed us. As I sent more shadows to conceal what was about to happen, I sensed Lucas and Kyler nearby. Rasher would've stayed inside, just in case. He played the role of sentinel so well, it was hard to consider he was an assassin.

Johan's hand found my waist, pulling me against him. I spun quickly, blade ready, no longer needing the pretense.

His eyes widened in recognition as my hood fell back. "You—"

He drew his sword with surprising speed despite his drunken state. Metal clashed against metal as I parried his first strike. Every glance at his face sent a new wave of fear through me, but I met him blow for blow, the need for vengeance urging me on. I was stronger than I was back then.

My dagger sliced his arm on the second pass, drawing a pained hiss from his lips. Blood dripped onto the cobblestones, black in the dim light of the moon.

He lunged forward, surprisingly quick for a drunk man. Pain exploded in my shoulder as his blade found flesh.

Ice crystals suddenly formed around Johan's feet, freezing him in place. Kyler emerged from the shadows, hands glowing with cold blue light.

Johan broke free with a curse, tumbling backward, but Lucas appeared behind him, the pommel of his sword raised.

It met its mark with a sickening crack. Johan crumbled to the ground, unconscious.

My hands shook as I stared at his still form, the man who had killed my grandmother, my only family, and my first love, now helpless at my feet. I raised my blade, preparing to end his life. The wails of the people I knew since childhood screamed in my head. The smell of smoke and ash lingered in the air. This is what I should've done that night. I don't know how, but he shouldn't have been allowed to live his life so carefree after such a decimation. I rehearsed this moment countless times, yet it proved unexpectedly simple. He would die while he was asleep, completely unaware of any pain, and therefore, saved in a twisted sense.

I lowered my hands and took a step back, my shoulder brushing against Kyler.

"You didn't kill him," he noted, his tone carefully neutral.

"Not yet," I wiped my blade clean on my leathers. "He doesn't deserve a quick death."

I motioned Lucas for help, already grabbing some rope that was discarded in the alley. We bound Johan's hands and feet, checking twice to ensure he couldn't escape. Kyler disappeared into the tavern only to return with Rasher, a cloth and more rope. He stuffed the cloth in Johan's mouth and tied the rope around his head, preventing him from spitting out his new gag. Rasher hoisted him over his shoulder like a sack of grain.

The inn was just beside the tavern, the old woman running it sat at the front desk waiting for weary travelers to come in search of lodging. Lucas went to acquire our room and distracted her as we snuck our victim past her. The back stairs creaked as we climbed to a hallway filled with rooms. Soft thuds against the worn wood signaled Lucas' approach, a triumphant grin stretched across his face as he shoved the key into the door. We hurried in, the door locking behind us with a satisfying click.

We dumped Johan in the corner, his head lolling against the wall.

Blood trickled down my arm from the wound Johan had inflicted. Kyler approached silently, his hand hovering over the cut. Ice formed beneath his palm, soothing the wound and numbing the pain.

"Oryn will be here soon." I checked the bindings once more, making sure they were secure. My stomach churned with anticipation at the thought of the confrontation to come.

CHAPTER 18

My heart pounded as a knock echoed through our room, three sharp raps that sent my pulse racing. The sound was like a death knell, marking the moment everything would change. One trauma from my past tied in the corner, another arriving.

Kyler's hand squeezed my shoulder before he stepped back, his touch lingering a moment longer than necessary. His eyes met mine, a silent promise that whatever happened next, I wouldn't face it alone.

I stood behind a small table we set up in the middle of the room, nodding at Rasher that I was ready. With Lucas and Kyler at my side, I was ready to face my husband.

Rasher opened the door, clearly sizing up the prince before allowing him entry. His golden hair was disheveled as if he'd been running his hands through it for hours, and he had dark circles under his eyes, opposite of the charming man I had met. The sight of him—so familiar, yet suddenly so foreign—made my chest ache with conflicting emotions. The dull pain from the thread between us being stretched taunt now completely vanished. Kyler had kept it from becoming as excruciating as it was, but despite an additional tether, the hurt from the separation from Oryn remained, just lessened.

His eyes widened at the sight of me, relief flooding his features. For a heartbeat, I remembered why I'd fallen for him once, the genuine warmth that had drawn me in like a moth to a flame.

That relief vanished when he spotted Kyler beside me. His blue eyes hardened to stone, his shoulders tensing beneath his fine tunic.

"What the fuck is he doing here?" Oryn growled, his voice a dangerous rumble. His hand instinctively moved to the sword at his hip.

He dropped my belongings on the floor with a thud—the items I'd requested as a pretense of luring him here. The sound punctuated the tension filling the room.

"Sit down," I pointed to the chair at the table, my voice calmer than my emotions.

Lucas and Kyler positioned themselves behind me, a united front of protection that made Oryn's eyes narrow further.

Johan stirred in his chair in the corner, dried blood smeared on his temple where he was struck. His eyelids fluttered, but he remained bound and gagged.

Rasher stood guard by the door, arms crossed over his massive chest, blocking the only exit. His expression remained neutral, but his eyes missed nothing.

Oryn's eyes darted between all of us, calculating. I could almost see the gears turning in his mind, assessing threats, planning escape routes. The warrior in him never rested.

"You have one minute to explain yourself," I said, fighting to keep my voice from trembling.

"Explain myself? I've been searching for you for months!" Indignation colored his words as he remained standing, refusing my command to sit. "The agony of leaving you the morning after our wedding was hard enough, it was our first day as husband and wife.

But it was like you became completely cut off from me and that's been shredding my soul. Then to return with news you were kidnapped... Do you have any idea... I was worried you were dead!"

The table between us felt like an ocean, vast and impossible to cross. Once, there had been nothing between us but trust and desire. Now, suspicion and betrayal created a gulf I wasn't sure could be bridged. A snake never strikes only once, and I despised snakes.

"Let's start with this: why make such an act of a love so grand it's a gift from the gods themselves, only to throw your supposed *lover* in a dungeon to be a mad man's play thing?" My voice barely rose above the whisper, but each word struck sharper than any sword.

The color drained from Oryn's face. "What dungeon? Alora, I swear—"

"Don't lie to me." I slammed my hand on the table, the sound cracking through the room like lightning. "I was imprisoned while you sat on your throne."

"I would never have done that to you," his voice broke, a crack in his perfect princely facade. "I've been out of my mind looking for you, Love. Kyler knew—"

"I only knew what you told me. But then I heard of what she went through." Kyler met my eyes as he spoke. "It's not something to take lightly, and she was told you were involved."

"It wasn't me."

"Then explain Souoak," Kyler demanded, his deep voice cutting through the tension.

Oryn fell silent, his jaw clenching. The muscle in his cheek twitched with barely contained rage.

"Sunnevean knights razed a town, slaughtering everyone. Your men recognized me only after almost killing me." Anger from the visions of the battle laced my words. "Why respect the princess consort if the crown prince himself doesn't care?"

"I wasn't there," Oryn whispered, his eyes never leaving mine. "I wasn't there at Souoak and I wasn't made aware of the attack until after they retreated," his eyes flicked to Kyler just for a moment only to return to mine. "I was looking for you. All I have done since I returned after leaving you in our bed was look for you."

The bond between us pulsed with his sincerity, that damn magical connection making it impossible to dismiss his words entirely.

A frustrated sigh left my mouth as I shook off the influence of the bond. It felt like I'm left with more questions than answers. The only thing I knew for certain was I would never be safe with him. I could never trust him or the bond.

"And what about him?" Oryn jerked his chin toward Kyler, jealousy radiating from him in waves.

Heat crawled up my neck, embarrassment and defiance warred within me. "What about him?"

"Don't play stupid, Lor. I can sense it through our bond." His voice dropped dangerously low. "I can *feel* what you've done."

I sensed a shift in Kyler's emotions. A steady calm began to bubble with rage. The temperature in the room dropped several degrees. I could only imagine the frost forming on his slender fingers, ready to send Ryn's way.

"Are you fucking him, too?" Oryn spat, his gaze shifted toward Lucas with pure contempt.

"I wish," Lucas snickered, unable to help himself even in this tense moment.

I cut Lucas a sharp look that promised retribution later.

Kyler and Oryn growled simultaneously, the sound so similar it might have been comical in any other situation.

"That's enough," I hissed, my patience worn thin. "You don't get to condemn me for doing what anyone else would have in my place. My mate betrayed me and another was presented, one who vowed his life and sword to me."

"Lor, I had no part in—"

I held my hand up, cutting him off. "Whether you were involved remains to be proven, but they were pretty eager to tell me you were well aware while they were taking what they wanted from my body while I was strapped to a table."

The last statement was like the final nail in a coffin. Oryn's protests and judgements ceased, and the room began to warm back to a normal temperature. Progress.

Oryn's eyes drifted to Johan, finally noticing the mercenaries' bound form. "What's he doing here?"

"Unfinished business," I said, gesturing to the bag of items left on the floor. Oryn grabbed the fabric and placed it on the table softly, pushing it toward me. I snatched it before his hand could brush my own and rooted around. All of my beautiful obsidian daggers, ready to be reunited with the one I had lost that Kyler returned, but what I really wanted was underneath them. I pulled the ancestral blade gifted by my grandmother from the bag and removed it from its sheath with a metallic hiss. The glittering blade sang a song that felt like the many days I spent running through the woods and helping in the garden. Starlight sparkled throughout its deadly blade.

I crossed to Johan in three quick strides, my movements fluid with purpose. The weight of the blade felt right in my hand, an extension of my will.

His eyes bulged as I pressed the blade to his throat, consciousness returning just in time for him to understand what was happening.

"Alora—" Oryn started, but made no move to stop me.

"You should've killed me when you had the chance," I whispered to Johan. "May the gods find your soul rotted and toss you into the void."

Blood sprayed as I sliced Johan's throat in one fluid motion, the hot crimson arc splattering across the floorboards. The sound of his final gurgle filled the room as his life drained away.

Lucas's jaw dropped, though he'd seen me kill countless times before. Perhaps it was the suddenness, the lack of hesitation.

Kyler remained impassive, his dark eyes revealing nothing of his thoughts.

Oryn didn't even flinch, his gaze steadied on mine as if measuring my resolve.

"Regretting marrying me yet?" I wiped my blade on Johan's shirt, leaving a dark smear across the fabric.

A smirk curled Oryn's lips, something dangerous and appreciative lighting his eyes. "I told you, I was interested in the woman who looked ready to fight someone. That includes stabbing, or really any sort of maiming. You'll have to try harder than that to sway me to ever regret marrying you, mate," he added, his voice dropping to a velvet purr.

"I'm just getting started," I stepped back, giving Kyler the signal we'd agreed upon.

Kyler moved behind Oryn, striking him unconscious with a swift blow. Oryn crumbled without a sound.

Before I could say a word, he began securing him. He must not be too upset with me for killing someone in front of him.

"Lucas, you know what to do."

Lucas helped me wrap Johan's body in sheets, his nimble fingers worked quickly. Blood soaked through the fabric, turning the crisp white a deep dark red.

"Messy, messy," Lucas tutted, though his eyes danced with amusement. "But very dramatic, especially for you. I approve."

Rasher entered from checking the hallway, shaking his head at the scene before him. "It's terrifying how normal this is for you two."

"I thought you took out all of Kyler's enemies for him," I chuckled. Surely the big man has done a clean up or two.

"Killed? Yes. Didn't care to tidy up the mess. Didn't stay long enough to consider it."

Lucas grinned, blood on his hands as he secured the makeshift shroud. "I always found a little murder between friends is just good ole bonding time."

CHAPTER 19

The gentle rock of waves made my stomach lurch as our ship cut through the dark waters. Two days at sea, and I still hadn't found my sea legs. Rasher found us a ship and a crew that turned a blind eye to the unconscious man we carried with us onboard in the dark hours of the morning. A man who, once he woke up, continued to badger me every time I went below deck. Between the seasickness and his anger, I chose to be ill more often than not.

Salt spray hit my face as I leaned against the Siren's Tear's rail, the bitter tang of it coating my lips. The endless expanse of water stretched before us, no land in sight. Captain Vallor, the ship's human captain, yelled orders to his men, who dutifully lumbered about. His bright copper hair blew in the breeze, his hat somehow staying atop his head. If I didn't know any better, I would've thought he was the god of the sea with his eyes glittering as he navigated the choppy waters, and his muscular dark arms holding the steer steady as he points ahead.

"Lift the sails! The wind's changin' and we best catch it." The unique timber and drawl of his words permeated the space. A chorus of "ayes" echoed around us.

"Never thought I'd see the day," I muttered, watching Lucas empty his stomach over the side for the fourth time that hour. The assassin who could slit throats without breaking a sweat and steal the coat off your back without your notice, reduced to this pitiful state.

He groaned, head hanging over the side, knuckles white where he gripped the wooden rail.

"I hate you all," Lucas whimpered, his usual charm nowhere to be found. His face had taken on a sickly pallor that made his eyes seem too large for his face.

"You know, for all the times I've seen you so drunk that you forgot how your legs worked, I never imagined you'd be taken down by a little water," I teased, though I felt a twinge of sympathy for his suffering.

Another wave rocked the ship, sending us tilting precariously to one side before righting itself.

"You're one to talk, Lor," Lucas turned greener, if that was even possible, and made a noise like a dying animal. "It seems I'm not the only one holding my head over the bow."

I try to retort, but the growing churn in my stomach has me leaning forward once again.

Below deck, chains rattled loudly, followed by a string of muffled shouts. My second problem of the day.

Oryn's cursing carried through the floorboards, colorful enough to make even Lucas blush on a good day.

"Someone shut him up," Rasher called from the helm, where he stood with the captain, discussing potential areas the islands could've been erased from the map in his hands.

"I'll do it," Kyler volunteered too eagerly, already moving toward the hatch and rolling his eyes.

I caught his arm as he passed me, stopping him. "No, I'll go."

His eyes drifted towards the hatch, unsure, his mouth drawn to a straight line.

"He's been at it for hours," Kyler protested, though he didn't pull away from my grasp. "Every time you speak, it's the same argument."

"I can handle him." I assured him, releasing Kyler's arm.

Lucas retched again, the sound pitiful and wet.

"After I handle that one," I added, patting Lucas's back sympathetically.

"I need you to follow through on the times you've threatened to kill me and do it now. Quickly, and nothing that marks my beautiful face so I can grace you with my beauty one final time before departing to the underworld." Lucas slumped against the rail, moaning with each rock of the boat.

"Don't be dramatic." I handed him water from the flask at my hip. "Small sips."

Kyler's eyes followed me as I crossed the deck, his gaze a physical weight between my shoulder blades.

The setting sun caught his face, gilding his features in the warm light, highlighting the sharp line of his jaw.

My heart skipped a beat, traitorous thing that it was. Once again, I found myself trying not to fall so fast for a mate. When he looked at me like I was the very world itself, or when his soft touch would find me in a moment where I was trapped in the torment of my thoughts, it was hard to deny that he was the steady presence I needed.

He raised an eyebrow, catching me staring.

Keep looking at me like that, Princess, and I'll have to order the crew to jump ship so I can spread you out on this very bow and listen to your sweet screams as you take every inch of me.

I ducked my head, hurrying below deck to hide what his words did to me. The warmth already spreading throughout my body begged me to go back and have him make good on that promise.

Stuffy air hit my face in the darkness of the hold, the thickness almost as suffocating as the proximity to the man who broke my heart.

"Come to check on your prisoner?" Oryn sneered from where he sat chained to a support beam.

I grabbed the tin cup set aside for him by a barrel of fresh water and dipped it in. I set the cup by his foot where he sat on the rough floor. He waited for my retreat before reaching towards it and took a slow drink. After the first time he tried to reach for me when I came to bring him food, he's learned I'm more willing to stay for a chat if he kept to himself.

"It's more than you bestowed upon me," I leaned against a post, keeping my distance.

He rattled his chains again, the sound grating against my nerves.

"These are unnecessary," he said, lifting his bound wrists.

"Are they?"

"I wouldn't hurt you," his voice softened, almost pleading.

"No, you just let others do it for you," I replied coldly.

"How many times do I have to say that I played no part in that? Had I known, I would've slaughtered every single one who dared to lay a hand on you. I swear to every lost god there ever was, Love. It. Was. Not. Me."

Silence fell between us, heavy with uncertainty.

Footsteps creaked overhead, reminding me I wasn't alone with my husband—my captor—my problem.

"I'll bring food later." I turned to leave, unable to bear the sadness that shone in his eyes.

"Alora—" he started, but I was already climbing back to the deck.

Lucas had finally stopped throwing up, I noticed with relief. He was curled up in a miserable ball against a crate, eyes closed.

Kyler stood at the bow, his tall figure silhouetted against the darkening sky. The wind whipped his dark hair as he stared out at the endless horizon.

I joined him, our shoulders touching lightly.

"You okay?" he asked softly, his voice barely audible over the waves.

"No," I admitted, the simple truth easier than pretending.

His fingers found mine, a reassuring squeeze telling me what he's told me almost every day since we bonded: I was safe, he was here, and I was safe.

Neither of us spoke. The silence stretched between us comfortably where it had been suffocating with Oryn.

The sun bled into the horizon, painting the sky in violent shades of crimson and gold.

Waves continued to crash against the bow, droplets of the cool water hitting my face, mingling with tears I refused to shed, the sea hiding my weakness as we sailed toward an uncertain future.

CHAPTER 20

That evening, Oryn was silent when I brought him food. I'm not sure what I expected, him to continue insisting his innocence? Begging for my forgiveness? Speaking of all the ways he loved me? All things he'd been forthcoming with since he awoke on the ship, words I thought I let brush by me with no hold on me. Their absence left a hole in my heart as I crawled onto the cot I shared with Kyler and drifted to sleep in his arms.

Moonlight filtered through the porthole, casting silver patterns across the wooden floor. My eyes snapped open, heart racing as if I'd been running. The ship creaked around me, a living thing breathing in the night.

"Alora," a familiar voice whispered from above.

I froze, recognizing the voice. It couldn't be, but all the same, I hoped for it. I sat up, careful not to wake Kyler as I snuck up to the bow.

I came face to face with the shimmering face of my grandmother. Translucent in the darkness, her form blurred at the edges like watercolor. Her spirit looked as I always remembered her, a simple gown and apron, dirty with dirt from the garden. Her grey hair woven into a single braid down her back. A serene smile greeted me.

"The path you walk is treacherous," she warned, eyes ancient and knowing.

"Yet, it seems it's what Fate demands," my soft steps halt before her ghost. A cry lodged in my throat at the very sight of the sweet woman who raised me.

"Aye, girl. You've got not much farther left. Your heart will lead you, trust it," she urged.

"My heart's been mistaken before." The words tasted like ash.

"Has it?"

The question hung between us, heavier than it had any right to be.

"He betrayed me," I insisted, voice breaking on the last word.

"Did he?" Her eyebrows rose, skepticism clear even in her spectral form.

"Stop speaking in riddles," I hissed, frustration bubbling up.

Her laugh echoed in my mind, familiar and sorely missed. "You were always stubborn."

The ship swayed beneath us, waves lapping against the hull in rhythmic patterns. Her wispy form flickered.

"I miss you," I whispered, tears began to stream down my face.

Her form began to fade, edges dissolving into the moonlight.

"Follow your heart, Lor, trust where it leads."

She disappeared like a morning mist, leaving me alone wishing for just one more moment. The captain had warned us when we boarded to be wary of the mysteries of the ocean, rambling on about being pulled out of the boat by demons and losing your mind. I knew I've been slowly losing my mind when I first began speaking with the Maël in my head. I would happily turn as crazy as the old witch if it meant being able to speak to Grandmother. Even if it was all in my head, hallucinations from being holed up in the boat for so long.

I slipped down below and padded across the wooden floor, following the tug that had been pulling me for weeks. Chains rattled in the darkness as I approached.

"Can't sleep?" Oryn asked, his silhouette barely visible in the gloom.

"Why did you do it? Please, stop holding back and just explain to me why." The words escaped before I could stop them.

"I didn't."

"Stop lying." I begged.

"I've never lied to you," he said quietly.

Something in his tone made me pause, a certainty that didn't match the narrative I'd constructed.

"Then help me understand," I demanded, crossing my arms.

"Would you believe me?" A genuine question, not a challenge.

Our bond pulsed faintly between us, a reminder of what we'd once shared.

"I don't know," I admitted.

He shifted in his chains, metal links clinking softly. "I was sent away by my father. When I returned, I was told you were taken. Kyler had already started investigating, searching. I left on my own search, hoping between the two of us you'd be found quickly."

"Until you stopped," I accused. Remembering the royal accounts of his activities I was shown.

"I never stopped." The raw pain in his voice caught me off guard. "I had to return to the palace to grab your things when you contacted me. I haven't been back since I finished searching it from top to bottom and started looking beyond it."

My resolve wavered, uncertainty creeping in where conviction had once been.

"I can't trust you," I said, but the words sounded hollow even to my ears.

"But you want to," he observed. Regret dawned on his face as he held up his hands in surrender. "At least, it feels like you do. What little I can feel while you have me shut out, that is."

"Wanting isn't enough." I swallowed hard.

"It could be."

I turned away, leaving his words hanging in the darkness.

CHAPTER 21

I woke to the violent rocking of the ship, my body nearly tumbling from the narrow bunk. The wooden beams above me groaned in protest as I grabbed the edge of my bed to steady myself.

"Get up!" Kyler's voice cut through the din, urgent and sharp. "Storm's hit."

I scrambled to my feet, steadying myself against the wall as the floor pitched beneath me. Through the small porthole, I caught glimpses of a sky turned pitch black, though it couldn't have been past midday.

"How bad?" I asked, yanking on my boots.

"Bad enough." His face was grim as he tossed me my shirt. "Captain's calling all hands."

We staggered up to the deck where chaos reigned. Rain lashed sideways, stinging my face like tiny needles. The sea heaved around us, massive swells lifting the ship before dropping it into valleys of churning water. Sailors scrambled across the deck, their movements desperate yet precise.

Captain Vallor stood at the helm, his massive frame braced

against the wheel as he bellowed orders. "Secure those lines! Drop the mainsail before it's ripped to shreds! Move your worthless asses!"

Lucas clung to the railing, his face a sickly shade of green that had nothing to do with the storm. "I hate the fucking ocean," he muttered.

"Less complaining, more helping," Rasher shouted, already moving to assist him with securing the rope Lucas clung to, with one hand to the rail.

A massive wave crashed over the starboard side, sending icy water flooding across the deck. I lost my footing, sliding across the slick wood until my back slammed against the mast.

"We're taking on water below!" A crewman shouted, his voice nearly lost in the howling wind.

Captain Vallor cursed. "We need every hand—"

The ship lurched violently, sending several men sprawling. A terrible cracking sound split the air as one of the smaller masts snapped, rigging whipping loose like angry serpents. It started to come down, heading towards a sailor working on the lot beside it until a spray of water erupted from Kyler's hand, pushing it overboard to save him.

My mind raced. There was one more pair of hands on this ship—capable hands currently bound in chains below deck.

"Kyler!" I called out, fighting my way toward him. "Can I trust him?"

His face darkened for a moment before understanding hit him. "I believe so. Why now?"

"Look around you!" I gestured wildly at the chaos. "We need more help or we're going to sink!"

Another wave crashed over us. Somewhere, a man screamed.

Kyler's jaw clenched, but he nodded.

We battled our way below deck, where seawater already was

sloshing around our ankles. Oryn sat alert in his chains, eyes sharp and assessing.

"Come to check if I've drowned yet?" he asked, though the usual bite was missing from his voice.

"We need your help," I said, pulling the key from inside my pants. "If this storm doesn't break soon, I'm worried we'll sink."

Surprise flickered across his face as I unlocked his shackles.

"You're trusting me?" he asked quietly.

"I'm trusting you want to live," I corrected, stepping back as he rubbed his wrists.

A tremendous crash overhead sent us all staggering. I lost my footing, sending myself towards the puddled floor until Oryn's firm hands caught me. Our bond sang with the brief moment of contact.

"We need to move," Kyler growled.

We raced back to the deck. The conditions had worsened. Captain Vallor was shouting for men to hold the lines.

"Where do you need us?" Oryn asked, voice carrying despite the storm.

The captain barely spared him a glance. "Help secure the rigging before it kills someone!"

We threw ourselves into the work, fighting against wind and water. Oryn worked tirelessly alongside us, his movements sure despite days spent in chains.

Hours blurred together as we battled the relentless storm. My muscles screamed in protest, hands raw and bleeding from the ropes. Yet somehow, we kept the ship afloat despite the abuse it suffered.

"Easy now, storms breaking!" Captain called, hollering more instructions to his men to take note of the damage and start repairs. He looked down at Kyler, Oryn, and me with a crooked grin on his face.

"You all have earned your sea legs today!" A large chuckle emitted from him.

"How is this thing not sunk?" Lucas sighed. He wiped his brow with worn hands, too exhausted now to let his sickness bother him.

"Aye, she's sturdier than ye think!" the captain crowed. "She's weathered storms worse than this a hundred times over." The pride in his ship did nothing to calm the churning in my stomach. My hand shook as I finally released my hold. A soft knock in my mind had my eyes meeting Oryn's pleading ones. I shook my head. I may have unchained him, but I was far from letting him breach another step past my resolve. Hurt flashed across his face as he took a timid step closer to me.

"Are you hurt?" he asked, holding his hand out.

I looked down at my bleeding hands. Rope burns and cuts covered them, but thankfully it was the worst of my injuries.

"I'm alright. Are you alright?"

A slight smile curved at his mouth. "Yeah, I am." He didn't appear as weighed down as he had when we spoke last night. Kyler cleared his throat in warning before pulling Ryn away to help him with assisting the crew.

Just as the wind began to ease, a strange stillness fell over the water around us. The waves calmed unnaturally, as if something massive moved beneath the surface.

"What the hell?" Lucas whispered, peering over the rail.

The water bulged upward, a dark shape rising from the depths.

Captain Vallor's face was drained of color. "Mother of gods..."

A massive, serpentine head broke the surface, towering above our ship. Cerulean scales gleamed along its body like sparkling gemstones. Bright orange eyes burning with pure malice.

CHAPTER 22

The sea serpent's massive head loomed above us, water cascaded from its scales not unlike the downpour we had only just survived. My stomach dropped as those burning orange eyes fixed on our ship—on us.

"Get to the cannons! Grab anything that wasn't blown overboard and prepare for battle!" Captain Vallor bellowed.

I reached for my daggers, though what good they'd do against something this size, I couldn't say. Beside me, Kyler summoned his ice magic, frost already forming around his fingertips. Rasher nocked an arrow while Lucas drew twin blades. A bow wedged between two barrels caught my attention. It'd be more effective than my blades. The only problem was those barrels were the closest things to the beast. But I was fast, maybe fast enough.

As I sprinted across the deck, Oryn's voice cut through the chaos. "Alora, stay back!"

The monster struck with terrifying speed, its massive head slamming into our port side. The ship lurched violently, sending several crew members flying. I grabbed the rope wrapped around the barrels to keep from falling, my knuckles white with effort. It struck close to my target, but thankfully not near enough to dislodge what I needed. I pulled the old bow out and found a quiver of arrows inside one of the barrels beside it. Now all I needed was a better vantage point.

"Aim for the eyes!" Kyler shouted, hurling spears of ice toward the creature's face. Flames erupted from Oryn as arrows and cannonballs littered the air, heading towards their formidable target.

I found a spot on the deck to brace myself while taking aim, sending an arrow towards the serpent's eyes. It sliced across the beast's scales. It barely seemed to notice.

The serpent reared back, preparing for another strike. Captain Vallor was shouting orders, directing his men to a massive harpoon mounted at the bow.

"We need to distract it!" I called to Kyler.

He nodded grimly. "I'll try to freeze its body to keep it from diving at us."

The monster lunged again, this time directly at me. I dodged, but its movement sent a wave crashing over the deck, sweeping me off my feet. I slid across the wet planks, scrambling for purchase.

"Alora!" Oryn's voice, desperate and raw, cut through the roars of battle.

The serpent's massive jaws opened wide, displaying rows and rows of razor-sharp teeth between two fangs as long as Kyler was tall. Before I could react, they closed around me.

Darkness. Wet, suffocating darkness.

I was inside its mouth. I was about to be fish food.

Panic clawed at my throat as I fought against the slick muscle, trying to push me deeper. The stench of rotting fish and death overwhelmed me. I couldn't breathe, couldn't think as I was thrown around the putrid space. Slamming into teeth, trying not to get caught between them.

I had lost my bow when I had tripped, my obsidian daggers likely too shallow to help in any way. I was never one to carry a sword, and that came to curse me in this moment. Its blade would've been long enough to do something. Anything.

I tried reaching for that blinding fire that flowed through my veins, but between my own fear of it and the living nightmare of being eaten alive kept me from grasping it.

My fingers found the hilt at my hip—the long dagger that served my ancestors. I pulled it from its sheath and starlight lit the cavernous maw that would send me to the afterlife. The sparkle a comfort in my final moments, hopefully a last hope to save my friends from meeting the same fate. With a desperate cry, I plunged it into the roof of the creature's mouth.

The beast's scream vibrated through my entire body. Its jaws opened in pain, and I was suddenly airborne, launched from its mouth into the open sky. The reprieve of fresh air almost brought a smile to my face.

For one suspended moment, I saw everything—our battered ship, my mates fighting below, and Captain Vallor at the bow, aiming the massive harpoon directly at the monster's eye.

Then I was falling, plummeting toward the dark sea.

The impact knocked the air from my lungs. Cold water enveloped me as I sank beneath the waves. Above, I heard the muffled explosion of the harpoon finding its mark, followed by the splintering crack of wood as the dying serpent crashed into the vessel.

I tried to swim upward, but my limbs felt like lead. My strength was gone, used up in that desperate fight for survival. Darkness edged my vision as my lungs screamed for air.

As consciousness began to fade, I reached upward one last time. Desperate to break through the rippling surface, to return to my companions who I begged any god who would listen to save. Take me if it means they would continue.

A strong hand closed around mine.

Through the murky water, I saw Oryn's face, determined and fierce as he pulled me toward the surface. Our bond, which I'd kept tightly closed, burst open with the force of his desperation.

Don't you dare leave me, Love. Not now. Not ever.

CHAPTER 23

We broke through the once wild tempest to calm waters. No sea serpent in sight. Pieces of the wreckage littered the surrounding ocean. I gasped, the fire in my lungs slowly easing as I waded in Oryn's embrace. His eyes searched my face, brows pushed forward with concern.

You saved me. I whispered into his mind.

I will always save you.

"Over here!" Lucas' voice called out. We turned to find him and Rasher floating on a large piece of deck.

Their faces were a relief. They were safe, alive. But there was another face missing, an important one.

"Where's Kyler?" I asked.

Water sprayed beside me as my missing mate emerged beside me. Seeing his face made me want to launch into his arms. To hell if it dragged me back underwater.

"Let's get on the raft before you're completely worn out." He said. Kyler's water magic swirled around the three of us, propelling us to our companions. My two mates helped me lift myself onto the thick wood before pushing themselves up to safety. The moment his knee gained purchase, Kyler grabbed me and pulled me close. His hand twisted into my hair and his lips crashed into mine, claiming me as if he was a conqueror on a new land.

"It's good to see you, too," I mused, leaving one last light kiss on his full lips before taking everything in around us. Rasher looked exhausted. Lucas was disheveled, but was less green than the last time I had seen him. Oryn sat beside me, looking anywhere but where Kyler's hands touched me. "Where's the crew? The captain?"

"Captain Vallor brought that thing down with a harpoon," Lucas told me. "But when the monster came down, it landed on the ship and sent all of us flying. This piece of the ship was by me when I came up. Rasher was floating not far away. Other than Kyler and now you two, we haven't seen sign of any other survivors."

No other survivors. After the storm and then the beast, how could only five of us make it? Maybe there were more, simply carried off by the current.

"Lets hope we find land soon." Kyler said, adjusting to look beyond to the horizon, bringing a jet of water to push us forward. We rode solemnly over the waves, our eyes keen to find even a small reprieve from the broken platform that held us.

By dawn, islands pierced through the morning mist ahead, dark shapes looming against the pink horizon. I stood transfixed in the center of our raft, the movement causing it to tremble with uncertainty. My breath caught in my throat.

"We made it," I breathed, eyes wide as I took in the scattered archipelago.

"Thank the fucking gods," Lucas sighed.

Kyler's magic pushed us faster, the tiny islands becoming larger before our eyes.

The Lost Isles sprawled before us, a cluster of scattered lands rising from the sea like the spine of some ancient beast. I counted at least four distinct islands of varying sizes. One rose dramatically with steep cliffs and what looked like a waterfall cascading down its face. Another appeared lush with dense jungle, while a third seemed barren and rocky.

"Look at them all," I whispered, mesmerized. "Which one do we choose?"

Kyler pointed to the closest island, shrouded in a blanket of fog so thick it seemed to pulse with its own heartbeat. "That one's closest. We need to get off this raft before it falls apart completely."

As we approached, the mist reached out like fingers, curling around our makeshift vessel. The temperature dropped, and I shivered, feeling Oryn's warmth press against my back instinctively. I didn't pull away.

"I don't like this," Lucas muttered. "It's too quiet."

He was right. No birds called. No insects hummed. Just the gentle lapping of waves against the shore as we beached our raft on the pale sand that disappeared into the fog.

"Stay close," Kyler commanded, drawing his sword. "We don't know what's waiting for us here."

Oryn channeled a flame into his palm. It wasn't much, but it helped keep the creeping chill at bay.

We ventured inland, the fog swirling around our ankles and climbing higher with each step. The ground beneath our feet changed from sand to stone, and suddenly, looming before us, the skeletal remains of what once might have been a grand structure.

"Gods above," Rasher breathed, reaching out to touch a crumbling column. "This looks older than anything I've seen in either kingdom."

We pushed deeper into the ruins, finding evidence of what must have been a thriving civilization—fallen archways, stone pathways, and the remnants of buildings that might have housed hundreds.

"We should make camp," Oryn suggested as the day's light began to fade. "I'll gather wood for a fire."

"I'll help," Lucas offered, still looking slightly green from our sea voyage. While on the dingy raft, he claimed his sickness was better than it had been on the ship. That optimism lasted mere minutes until he was back to being miserable. I didn't even have the heart to tease him about telling Vanya about his newfound weakness. With my luck, he'd finally achieve making her angry enough to do something, and I wouldn't put it past her to have him strapped to the bow of a ship for months on end.

While they worked, I explored a little further with Kyler, finding a courtyard that offered some shelter from the elements. We flagged down our companions to show them the spot before we went in search of food. By the time we returned, Oryn had built a fire, and Rasher was laying out what he could find for supplies. Rasher had better luck than we did, he had a few fish roasting on the fire that would were far better fare than the small fruits we could find.

"This isn't so bad," Oryn said, leaning back and looking up at the stars now visible through the breaks in the fog. "Sleeping under the stars, adventure on the horizon. Reminds me of our hunting trips."

Kyler snorted. "Except this time you were kidnapped and not high off some mushrooms you confiscated from a knight."

"Details," Oryn waved dismissively. Clearly not bothered by how we brought him on the ship. In many ways, the man was an enigma, but his definition of socially acceptable behavior rivaled even Lucas. "I'd rather you drag me along than leave me behind. We've got some things to work through, but we're all stuck together now, aren't we? Might as well make the best of it."

His words twisted my stomach into knots. He wasn't wrong—we were bound together, the three of us, by the highest of powers. But I remained convinced that breaking my bond with Oryn was the only path forward, the only way to reclaim my freedom, even as doubt flickered in the shadows of my mind.

CHAPTER 24

Dawn broke through the thinning fog, casting long shadows across the ruins. I'd barely slept, too aware of both Kyler and Oryn breathing nearby, too conscious of the strange energy that pulsed through this forgotten place.

My boots crunched on broken tiles as we explored the area surrounding our camp. Ancient paths wound between ruins, some were barely visible beneath centuries of growth, others were still remarkably intact.

"These markings," I murmured, tracing my fingers along the stone walls that seemed to hum beneath my touch. The symbols carved into the stone were unlike any language I'd seen before—fluid lines that curved and connected in patterns that made my eyes want to follow them endlessly.

I gasped when they pulsed faintly under my touch, a soft blue light illuminated my fingertips.

Kyler's hand brushed my shoulder, warm and steady. "Look ahead," he said quietly.

Beyond the scattered ruins we'd been exploring stood something impossible—a massive structure looming intact against the morning sky. White marble gleamed despite its age, untouched by time or the elements, as if it had been built yesterday rather than centuries ago.

Columns rose like silent guardians around its perimeter, each one carved with the same flowing script that had lit beneath my fingers.

"A temple," Rasher whispered, coming to stand beside us, his expression filled with awe.

Wide steps led to bronze doors that towered at least fifteen feet high, their surfaces etched with constellations I recognized from childhood stories.

Lucas whistled low. "Still standing after all this time. It doesn't make any sense."

Oryn stopped beside Kyler, his eyes fixed on the structure with the same wonder reflected in all our faces.

My hand pushed against the door almost of its own accord, and the metal yielded with surprising ease, swinging inward without a sound.

White flames flickered in sconces along the walls, casting dancing light across the marble floor.

"That's not natural," Lucas backed away a step, eyeing the flames with suspicion.

I exchanged a glance with Kyler and Rasher before reaching toward the nearest sconce. Heat radiated from the flames without burning my skin. The color alone looked like the power I couldn't control. These seemed docile in comparison.

A song whispered in my mind, soft notes pulling me forward into the temple's depths. "Do you hear that?" I asked, turning to the others.

Blank faces met my question. Whatever called to me, they couldn't hear it.

The melody grew stronger with each step, guiding me deeper. My feet followed marble halls as if they knew the way, passing faded artwork that covered the walls, stories told in faded paint that seemed to shift when viewed from the corner of my eye.

Double doors towered ahead, more grand than the entrance, gold leafing peeled from carved wood that depicted scenes of stars falling to the land. They swung open at my touch, a dark creak echoed in the chamber beyond.

My breath caught as a grand hall stretched endlessly before me, columns reaching to a vaulted ceiling so high it disappeared into shadow. Starlight streamed through windows, casting patterns across the floor—but it was still morning outside.

The song pulsed in my blood now, no longer gentle but an insistent beating drum as steps led to a raised dais at the hall's center.

There sat a throne.

Stars themselves seemed woven to form its structure, light bending around it in ways that hurt my eyes. Reality warped nearby, the air shimmering like heat over desert sand. The cosmos trapped in metal and stone, ancient power radiating outward.

My heart pounded faster as I approached, drawn forward by something that felt old and familiar all at once. The song reached a crescendo in my mind as the throne called to me, white flames dancing higher in their sconces as stars pulsed in rhythm with my heartbeat.

CHAPTER 25

I stood transfixed before the throne that mirrored the night sky, unable to look away from its cosmic beauty. My body hummed with recognition, as if every cell knew this place, knew this moment had been waiting for me.

Alora.

Kyler's voice filled my mind, warm and hesitant, wrapping around my thoughts like a gentle embrace.

I made sure that door that connected me with Oryn is closed before responding. *We feel so close. This place feels right.*

I could feel his hesitation through the bond. *Are you sure this is right? He saved you, and he sounded earnest when you confronted him. When you went missing, he told me he was searching the few times we communicated.*

Did you see him looking the entire time? Can you say without a doubt he played no part in my harm?

I cannot. He spoke with reluctance. *I was alone on my search and then found myself dragging you to Esmeray. But I have known him for a long time, I've heard him lie his way out of plenty of things. His words sounded earnest.*

I didn't respond, not wanting to consider the alternative. Since the Alchemist alluded to Oryn's involvement, I'd done nothing but grieve and let go of the relationship I thought I would have with my mate, my husband. It felt like a blessing that Kyler could be bonded to me in the same way. The senile witch gave me the key to moving forward from the trauma of being tied to Oryn for all of eternity.

What happens after this is done?

My heart skipped at his question, at the vulnerability laid bare before me. The mental bond between us pulsed. It still felt new, almost raw.

Images flashed unbidden—a future painted in soft morning light, his smile across the training yard, peaceful moments stolen between duties, his hand in mine as we walked through celebrations with his people happy and liberated. Where the war was finally put to rest.

I... I want a life with you. I projected back, letting him sense the truth of it.

His breath caught audibly behind me, the sound echoed in the vast chamber.

A real life. I understand we didn't join in the most traditional manner, I continued, my thoughts flowing freely to him. *But I don't want to only be tied together because you took pity on me and agreed to help me with this. I want to stand beside you, just as you have for me.*

His thoughts flooded with hope and fear, a chaotic swirl that mirrored the stars in the throne before us.

You mean that? His mind whispered, disbelief threading through his question. I couldn't blame him. I was clear this was an arrangement on my end and never promised anything more. It didn't matter whether it was the natural pull to love him or all the ways he's proven his devotion to me since we started on this hair-brained scheme. I knew when this was all over, I wanted my days spent with him. Even if it meant picking a fight.

Every word.

Oryn shifted uncomfortably nearby, clearly sensing the conversation he was kept out of. His eyes darted around the chamber as he came to my other side, brow furrowed.

"Something's not right here," he muttered, voice tight with unease.

The throne pulsed brighter at his words, as if responding to his doubt. Stars swirled in its frame, faster now, constellations formed and dissolved in heartbeats.

My feet carried me forward without conscious thought, drawn by an invisible thread. Each step echoed in the hall, the sound bounced off the high walls.

Power thrummed through the ancient stone beneath my boots, vibrating up through my legs, and settled its claws deep in my chest.

"A throne of stars," I breathed, the words hardly more than a whisper as I recalled them.

My hand reached out, fingers stretching toward the glittering light. Something called to my blood. It felt like the first time I intentionally used my shadows.

"Alora, don't!" Kyler's voice broke through the chamber, desperation cut through our mental bond.

His footsteps rushed toward me, a frantic rhythm against the marble. Oryn lunged forward, both men moved in unison despite the tension between them.

They both reached for my arm, fingers grasping at empty air as my fingertips brushed the cold starlight.

Shadows leached from me, curling around us and the throne. Reality bent.

The room warped around us.

Light fractured, darkness pulsed.

Flesh and stone seemed to twist and swirl.

The world shifted beneath our feet.

CHAPTER 26

W hite light exploded around us, so bright it seemed my skin might burn away. I squeezed my eyes shut, but the brilliance penetrated even through closed lids, turning my vision crimson.

Once the light faded and the dizziness subsided, a figure appeared upon the throne. Where emptiness had been moments before, now sat a being beyond anything I had seen before. A dark cloak covered the figure, even its hood hung low over its face. Sharp points circled its head beneath the hood, like a deadly crown adorning the temple. Thin, bone like fingers rested on the throne's arms. Despite his shrouded appearance, a formidable essence permeated the air with the being's presence.

My knees buckled under its overwhelming power that filled the chamber. I fell forward, catching myself on my palms against the cold stone floor. The air grew heavy, pressing down on my shoulders like physical weight.

The newcomer lounged sideways across the star-studded seat, one leg draped casually over the armrest.

"Well, well. My little champion has finally arrived." Their voice echoed like broken glass, each syllable sharp enough to draw blood. "Did you come to thank me for all that I have bestowed upon you?"

"I'm not your anything," I spat, pushing myself back to my feet despite the crushing pressure. Oryn and Kyler stepped closer to me, tense and ready to pounce at a moment's notice. "Why would I thank you when I don't know you?"

Their laugh cut through the chamber, the sound ricocheted off ancient walls and piercing my eardrums. I fought the urge to cover my ears.

"Oh darling, you've been mine since birth." They examined their fingernails with casual interest. "Quite bold to argue as a mortal face to face with Death itself. Especially when I recall hearing you tell your rivals in the past that you would greet me like an old friend. I expected a warmer welcome from you, Champion."

My stomach dropped, insecurity settled where my courage had been moments before.

"Your ability to rid the world of any soul? The shadows that bend to your will?" Death's head cocked to the side. I imagined a sinister smile spreading across the face I couldn't see. "My gifts, freely given."

I felt Kyler's presence burn behind me, his alarm and anger pulsed through our bond. His hand found my shoulder, steadying me.

"The witch sent me here. She said you were able to help me." I said, forcing strength into my voice.

"Yes, yes," Death waved their hand at me. "Fate's witch, my sister, always enjoyed driving *her* chosen one mad with riddles. Though, I'm not sure I can help you beyond what I have already done for you. Are you not satisfied to hold dominion over how long a being may exist?"

"The witch said I could break a bond if I came here with another to replace it."

Oryn's sharp intake of breath pierced me like a physical blow. "You can't mean that," he whispered, his voice broken.

Death clicked his tongue, the sound was like bones snapping. "Foolish child."

They leaned forward, starlight rippling across their form as they moved. "Did you think you could outrun Fate?"

"The witch—"

"You misunderstood," he cut me off before I could utter another word. "No god or being can change a mate bond. Fate herself cannot alter what has already woven in the stars."

"I can't accept that," I growled, standing taller.

"Can't or won't? You're smarter than this. The call of revenge shall not be put before the wills of the gods," Death said.

My fists clenched at my sides. "It's not revenge."

"Fine, then how much longer will you punish your mate before you accept the truth?"

"I have lived through the truth."

Death rose from the throne, power crackled around them like lightning. "My champion, drowning in denial and too stupid to see it."

His form flickered, momentarily revealing something ancient and terrible beneath his cloak. "Those bonds are written in the stars. They are sacred, capable of things most wouldn't understand."

"I don't care."

"Accept the path bestowed upon you. There are far more things at stake and there's no time for your whining."

Tears burned my eyes, but I refused to let them fall. "Haven't I done enough? Why chain me to someone who betrayed me? Do the gods find the pain they cause sacred?"

Death circled us slowly, his presence leaving trails of cold in the air. "Bonds are made to be the only things capable of strengthening you. Betrayal is not possible." He stopped in front of me, so close a mere shift would have me brushing against the cloth that covered him. "You've asked if you've done enough when you haven't accepted your path, your destiny. Every kill, every soul that crossed your path, your natural skills that have helped you along the way. That was *me* guiding you, preparing you for what was to come." Their fingers traced my cheek, a touch colder than ice. "You were meant for greater things."

Ice spread through my veins at their touch, freezing me from the inside out.

"Stop denying what you are. Stop fighting your destiny."

I felt Oryn's pain bleeding through our bond, raw and unbearable.

Death returned to their throne, settling back into the cosmic seat with fluid grace. "The bonds remain."

CHAPTER 27

Death's eyes flashed, shifting from starlight back to void. For someone who didn't show their face, their expressions were not absent. His body language was clear that he had more to say.

"Now that we have settled that, let's focus on the important matters."

"Important matters?"

"Yes." A bony finger thumped on the arm of his seat. "One does not come to Runerth unless things are dire. And my dear little wraith, things are dire."

My breath caught in my throat. "What do you mean?"

"Life's champion has fallen, and if you're not careful, you'll be next." He halted the ministrations of his finger. "Your grandmother held the very essence of life. That essence now must find a suitable host, but that won't stop what's already begun."

My brows pulled together. None of this made sense. Grandmother? Life's champion? "I don't understand."

"The balance shifts dangerously." Death slammed a fist down on the stone. Their outline blurred at the edges as their form began to fade into the surrounding darkness. "The scales tip toward Chaos, and you must stop it. They seek to take that which they have not been given."

"Wait!" I lunged forward, reaching for answers that dissolve like mist between my fingers. "You can't just—"

"Choose wisely, little champion." His voice lingered after his form had nearly vanished. "Your path forks before you. Each choice decides the fate of us all. Wield your destiny as you were always meant to."

The starlight dimmed around us, its brilliance faded to ordinary darkness. Reality snapped back, throwing me off balance. The chamber spun violently, and my knees hit the cold stone as I collapsed. My stomach lurched with the sensation of being wrenched back into my proper place in the world. The throne was no longer alight like a supernova. It sat with its faint glimmer, as if waiting for Death to sit upon its surface once again.

Rasher's hands gripped my shoulders, steadying me as I swayed.

"Lor! Can you hear me?" His voice sounded muffled, as though shouting at me through water.

Lucas paced frantically nearby, hands raking through his hair. "What the fuck just happened? One second you were touching that chair, then you were just... catatonic. All three of you, staring at empty space and not responding."

My head spun as I processed his words. Death, I met the god of death. He said I was practically made by him, a champion of what I still didn't understand. The balance... chaos... Each thought hammered against my skull like physical blows. Oryn, I was never going to be able to break our bond.

Kyler steadied himself against a pillar, his face ashen. He'd seen it too. Felt it.

Oryn's face twisted with rage as he stood. Without warning, he stormed past us without a word, shoulders rigid with fury.

His footsteps echoed through the empty halls as he disappeared into the shadows.

Lucas helped me stand, his arm strong around my waist. "What's his problem?"

"Me, I'm the problem," I sighed. "He found out I brought him here to break our bond."

Lucas whistled low. "Yeah, I'd say that went well," he quipped, though his voice lacked its usual humor. "So, is it just you and grumpy over there now?" He nodded towards Kyler, who shot him a vicious look.

"No." Tears welled in my eyes as reality settled in. "We need to figure out how to get back."

"If what Death said is true, we have bigger problems to worry about." Kyler wrapped an arm around me, pulling me into his side and out of Lucas's arms. "It'll be okay, Princess," he whispered low for only me to hear. I wished I could believe that, but it all felt so far from being alright.

The temple felt hollow now, drained of the power that had hummed through its walls just moments before.

Our steps quickened toward the exit, we told Rasher and Lucas about our meeting with Death along the way. Cool air hit my face as we emerged, the dense fog now seemed more ominous than before.

Oryn was already halfway to shore, his back rigid, his strides purposeful.

Lucas stumbled on loose stones, cursing under his breath. "Do you miss regular old assassin work? Just stab them and bag them. Not being a plaything for the gods." He asked me.

Kyler bristled at his words. My poor mate was still growing accustomed to his new closeness to the darkness of our craft he had sworn to dispel.

I didn't have time to respond before Rasher and Kyler began discussing our way off this island. Neither one of them coming up with an idea that could realistically take us the distance we needed to go. I watched Oryn march further away from us. Desire to chase after him, to take it all back flared within me, but I knew I couldn't go.

A rustling in the trees sent the hairs on the back of my neck up. Lucas and I turned in time to see a young man, no older than sixteen. His tawny skin and long black hair were the perfect canvas for his hazel eyes to shine. He bowed before us, causing my friend's brow to raise and our other companions to approach.

"Who are you?" I asked.

The man held his head high with confidence despite the tension that grew among us with the mysterious company.

"I am one with the island, one with the sea. The gods spoke to me and I must aid you."

"Aid us?" Kyler questioned.

"You have no boat," he gestured towards the empty waters. "My people can help you return to your lands."

I glanced around. Normally, I would've assumed this was a ruse. The gods sending someone to help? After witnessing a god in the flesh, I wasn't so quick to dismiss the man's words.

"Lead the way," I said. And we silently followed another gift Death has blessed us with.

CHAPTER 28

The island man led us through dense vegetation until we reached a clearing where thatched huts formed a neat circle around a central fire pit. Children playing with wooden toys stopped to stare. Women grinding grain paused, hands hovering over stone bowls.

"Outsiders," someone whispered in the common tongue before they returned to their own language. Their R's rolled and an accent I've never heard of flowed with their words.

An elderly woman approached, her face a map of wrinkles, eyes sharp as a hawk's. She spoke to our guide, who responded with animated gestures toward the temple we'd left behind.

The old woman's expression darkened. She looked at me directly, her gaze unsettlingly perceptive.

"You disturbed the sacred place," she said, her thick accent grounded each syllable.

"We didn't mean to," I answered, guilt washing over me.

She studied me again, then nodded once. "The spirits speak through you. Come. Eat. Rest."

The villagers welcomed us cautiously, offering bowls of fragrant stew and fresh bread. Children peeked at us from behind their mothers' skirts. Oryn sat apart, accepting the food with a stiff nod but not speaking to those who looked on him curiously.

"We need to return to our homeland," Kyler explained to the wise woman. "Our ship was destroyed."

The woman nodded gravely. "The waters grow angry. The balance shifts." Her gaze found mine. "You feel it too." She pointed towards her heart. "Here."

I swallowed hard. "Yes."

"We can help you return," she said, gesturing to several young men nearby. "My sons will prepare our trading vessel."

"We're grateful," Rasher said, bowing his head respectfully.

The elder leaned closer, her voice dropping. "But heed my warning—stay far from the rocky island to the east. Evil spirits taint that land. Those who step on its shores never return."

By morning, a sleek vessel waited at the beach, its sails emblazoned with symbols I didn't recognize. A small crew of men loaded provisions, their movements efficient and practiced.

Rasher helped Lucas aboard, steadying him as the boat rocked.

"Next time, less sailing and no gods," Lucas muttered, already looking green around the edges.

Kyler's hand found mine, his touch grounding me as the island began to disappear in the mist behind us.

Lor, his calming voice murmured into my mind. *We should talk about what happened.*

I nodded numbly, unable to form words as we departed the place that changed everything.

Oryn retreated below deck acknowledging none of us, his pain a tangible thing even without our bond wide open. I thought being separated from him hurt, but nothing could have prepared me for what I felt in this moment. Cutting out my own heart felt like a reprieve compared to the despair that had begun to constrict around me, cutting off my air.

My bonds pulsed with tension—one hot with anger, the other warm with reassurance.

Lucas leaned over the railing, looking miserable. "At least Death didn't kill us," he offered weakly.

Rasher smacked the back of his head.

CHAPTER 29

Salt spray stung my face as I stood on deck, watching the endless blue stretch before us. The voyage back from the Lost Isles had been mercifully quick but unbearably tense. Ryn hadn't met my eyes in days, not since the temple. Not since Death. Not since I'd made my demand to sever our bond.

The pain burning in my chest reminded me of what I felt when our connection stretched too thin. Was this my life? Staying close enough to the fae prince who now truly hated me to avoid being hurt by the very thread that binds me to him? Kyler at my side did help, but it never fully erased what I had experienced. I was doomed for all of eternity.

Did the gods find joy in chaining me to the male I was so sure let me rot under his orders? If they were all like Death, I'd say the misfortune of mortals was as entertaining as a noble's gossip. Mayhem to distract oneself until the next scandal came. A vice gripped my lungs. I was trapped and had angered my captor. If Oryn was capable of that while pretending to love me, what was he going to do now that he openly loathes me?

The mainland emerged through the morning haze, a dark

smudge on the horizon gradually taking shape into the familiar coastline. The specks moving in the distance were likely the worn boats arriving with wares to Saints Landing. My heart twisted with each ignored glance from Oryn, each time he deliberately turned away when our paths crossed on the small vessel. Only to remind myself I shouldn't be so bothered. I wanted to be rid of him, right?

The port bustled with morning commerce as we approached—fishermen hauling in their early catches, merchants setting up stalls, dock workers shouting instructions. We docked among fishing vessels, our ship conspicuous only in its plainness.

Kyler's hand steadied my elbow as we disembarked, his touch gentle but firm.

"Keep your hood up," he murmured, eyes scanning the crowd. "We don't want to draw attention to ourselves."

The market square teemed with people going about their daily business, oblivious to the war brewing in the east, to the games set by the gods, and to the turmoil inside me. Fish mongers cried their wares, the smell of fresh catch mingled with baking bread and spices.

Sweat trickled down my neck beneath my heavy cloak as we wove through the press of bodies. The crowd pressed close, jostling us from all sides. A sudden push into Rasher was enough for my cloak to be caught. My hood fell back from my face, exposing me.

Sunlight hit my violet eyes as Oryn and Kyler both spun towards me, Oryn's hood fell with his sudden movement.

Someone gasped. "Prince Oryn is here!"

Whispers rippled through the crowd like wind through tall grass, gaining volume with each passing second.

"Look, that must be the princess consort."

"She's returned!"

Hands reached toward me—some reverent, some merely curious. Oryn's arm circled my waist protectively, pulling me against him as

Lucas and Rasher pushed through bodies ahead of us. Kyler was close behind me, blocking us from the rear.

"Make way!" Lucas shouted, his voice carrying authority despite his slender frame.

Flowers were thrown at Ryn and me, a surreal detail amid the chaos. Children pointed and stared, some being lifted onto shoulders for a better view of the royal couple.

Rasher's bulk parted the crowd ahead of us, creating a path where none existed before. I caught sight of Ryn's face—his jaw clenched tight, expression unreadable. At first I didn't understand why he hadn't reached for me first, but I'm sure it would lead to a scandal if Kyler was the one with his arm around me. I could practically see the headlines now: "Princess Consort and the Prince's Guard: A Secret Affair". I'm sure it was bad enough he was forced to touch me, to be so close to my orbit, as we waded through the streets. He wouldn't want to deal with more drama on top of it.

Sweat beaded on my forehead as panic threatened to overwhelm me. An alley appeared to our right, narrow and shadowed.

Kyler pushed us through the opening, away from grasping hands and curious eyes. My back hit the cool stone as we pressed close, letting my shadows out to give us extra coverage. Unless someone came this way, we'd remain hidden.

Ryn eyed me with a raised eyebrow and I realized my mistake immediately. He witnessed me kill a man right in front of him, didn't bat an eye. But he had never seen me wield any power, and I just showed my hand. Lucas peered around the corner, assessing our situation.

"Well, that's fucked," he muttered, running a hand through his hair.

Rasher kept watch at the alley's mouth, his massive frame blocked most of the entrance. "We can't stay here."

Ryn's voice cut like ice when he finally spoke. "Word will reach the capital soon. Which means my father will not only be aware of where I am and send messengers to call me back, but he'll know we've reunited."

My stomach dropped at the implications. We'd lost any chance of approaching Sunneva quietly.

"We have no choice," I said, voicing what we all knew.

Kyler's fingers squeezed mine, a silent reassurance. "We'll figure it out."

Lucas kicked a crate in frustration, sending it skidding across the cobblestones. "Back to the viper's nest, then."

Rasher nodded grimly. "We'll leave at nightfall."

The alley felt smaller by the second, closing in around us like a trap. My bonds pulsed with dread.

Ryn draped his hood over his head once again and disappeared into the crowd without another word, his strong back the last visible thing before he became one with the throng of people.

The capital awaited.

CHAPTER 30

We managed to stay hidden until the sun descended from the sky. I watched as Rasher and Lucas mounted their horses, the beasts stamping impatiently outside a shabby stable just beyond the Saints Landing gates. They'd take a different route—less conspicuous than the carriage Oryn left to acquire for us.

"You can stay at the old bookshop in the capital square," I whispered, keeping my voice low enough that only they could hear. "There's a loft up top with a window that faces the rear. Lucas should be able to open it. We'll send a message when we can. Hopefully, I'll be able to meet you there shortly after our arrival."

Lucas winked, his usual playfulness returning despite the gravity of our situation. "Don't miss me too much, Lor. Try not to have too much fun while I'm gone."

Kyler rolled his eyes at his antics, a thoughtful improvement from the growls they'd usually illicit.

Their horses disappeared down the dirt path that led through the desert, the soft thump of hooves a steady beat that faded as their figures shrunk in the distance. I tugged my hood lower, now overly cautious of anyone who passed by. I leaned into Kyler, a sigh escaped that I didn't realize I had been holding.

What's on your mind, Princess? His voice came through the bond, steady as we kept our eyes ahead.

Is it really necessary for us to travel like this? I'd rather be on a horse...my own horse.

The king has eyes everywhere and would expect you both to be in a carriage. If it were just Oryn and me, horses would've been acceptable, but the two of you traveling together—anything less would be unacceptable and it doesn't serve us to evoke his ire.

He hates me, truly hates me. I'm not sure how this will work.

Alora, I don't know a single male who would have a different reaction to learning their mate wanted to be rid of them. I would tear through time and space to stay connected to you.

I chuckled down the bond. *What happened to giving me a choice?*

I gave you your choice, and you chose me even when I warned you it was irreversible. I'm not sorry to say you're stuck with me for all eternity now, Princess.

There are worse fates. My words brought a somber feeling that draped over me. *Maybe Ryn and I can keep from killing each other before we arrive.*

I have no doubts you two will be fine. After your display with Johan, I think we all know who would win in a fight. Ryn has enough self preservation to realize that. A chuckle rumbled through the bond that I couldn't help but smile at.

Minutes later, a carriage appeared beside us, pulled by speckled steeds. My stomach twisted at the sight. The door opened and Ryn stepped out. His golden hair caught the light as he extended his hand to help me up.

"My lady," he said formally.

The surprise I felt that he was addressing me, even looking at me, dissipated. Of course it was an act, a mask so easy to wear until he could drop it.

His touch burned through my gloves, the bond between us pulsed despite my efforts to keep it closed. I stepped into the carriage, careful not to meet his eyes.

Kyler's stallion pranced beside us, the massive beast as dark as midnight. He would follow. I wasn't truly alone with the prince.

The carriage door clicked shut with terrible finality. Ryn sat across from me, his tall frame filled the space, making it impossible to forget his presence. Velvet cushions pressed against my back, soft and suffocating.

"They'll expect a story," Ryn said after a long silence, his voice neutral.

My fingers twisted in my lap. "Tell them someone kidnapped me. Isn't that already the narrative?"

His eyes narrowed, the blue in them turning to ice. "It is, but by whom?"

I shrugged. "Mercenaries from the north."

The carriage wheels rattled over uneven terrain as we moved through the desert that surrounded Saints Landing. Just a few days in this heat and we'd finally hit the rolling plains. A few more days and we'd be at the palace steps.

"Tell them Kyler found me in Esmeray." I risked a glance at him. "He sent word to you and you came to ensure my safe return."

"I suppose that would be enough." His voice was flat, almost disbelieving. "And what will you say?"

"I missed my husband and am thankful to be reunited with him." The words tasted like ash on my tongue, the tightness in my chest held a bit of truth within them.

Ryn's jaw worked, muscles tensing beneath his skin. "Are you now?"

I met his eyes, pushing any emotions down beneath the surface. "If that is what we need me to be, then that is what I am." I kept my tone neutral.

His eyes softened slightly. "We'll need to be convincing. If they suspect anything then they will descend on us like rabid wolves."

My nails dug into my palms as I gazed out the window, watching Kyler's horse gallop alongside us. My heart ached to be on that horse with him, the breeze whipping through my hair, nothing but miles of open trail to explore.

"I know how to pretend."

The carriage hit a bump, I lurched forward. Our knees brushed, and I jerked back as if burned. His face hardened again, the momentary warmth vanishing.

"Do you?" For a moment, with a hint of teasing in his tone, he sounded like the Ryn I'd known before—before everything went wrong.

Kyler's shadow passed the window, his vigilant presence the only thing keeping me grounded. "I learned from the best."

Ryn flinched as if I'd struck him.

Silence filled the space between us, heavy and oppressive.

The remainder of our journey continued with the same pattern of silence, strained comments, and a mutual desire to be anywhere but riding in this carriage together. There were times I sensed his gaze upon me, only to look and find him looking out the window.

Days later, the city walls finally loomed ahead, with imposing stone barriers that gave citizens the comforting sense of protection. But now they felt like prison walls.

Guards snapped to attention when we approached, recognizing Kyler as he gave orders as we rode through town.

"Ready?" Ryn asked, adjusting his collar.

I straightened my spine, lifting my chin. "Always."

The palace gates creaked open, the sound echoing in my chest. Kyler sent reassurance down the bond, the only thing he could do while prying eyes surrounded us.

The castle rose before us, its spires reaching toward the sky like claws. Beautiful and insidious—I had returned to my gilded cage.

CHAPTER 31

The palace doors swung open, revealing a sea of nobility that had gathered in the grand hall. Servants had rushed ahead to announce our arrival, and now dozens of eyes scrutinized our every move. I fixed my face into the mask I'd worn so many times before—devoted to their prince and his kingdom.

"Smile," Ryn whispered, his hand found the small of my back. "They're watching."

I did as instructed, leaning slightly into his touch as we descended the marble staircase. The touch of his hand sent unwanted warmth through me, the bond between us humming despite my effort to ignore it. I had expected him to stiffen at my approach, but to my surprise, he appeared to relax, his fingers moving slightly enough to sense a gentle tug towards him. After figuring out our story, there was not much else said. The only good thing about stepping foot inside the palace was escaping the discomfort of the carriage. As confident as I was in maintaining a facade to get to the end result, I was losing faith in our ability to work together.

Kyler trailed behind us, the perfect picture of a dutiful royal guard. His face betrayed nothing, but I sensed his tension through our bond. I fought the urge to look back at him for the comfort I needed. It was weird to have found that in him, but it was a reprieve I was grateful for at a time like this.

"He's found the princess," someone whispered, loud enough for me to hear.

"She doesn't look like someone who was stolen… maybe she tried to run away after all."

Another voice answered, "She looks different. Something in her eyes…"

I kept my smile firmly in place, ignoring the whispers that followed us like a plague. The nobles parted before us, some bowed deeply, others offered stiff nods. I recognized the faces from my time at court—some concerned, others calculating, and a few openly hostile.

Glad to see nothing's changed in my short time away.

The King of Sunneva waited at the end of the hall, seated upon his ornate throne. His crown glinted in the light that streamed through the stained glass windows, his face was an unreadable mask of royal dignity.

"Father," Ryn said, bowing his head slightly.

The king's eyes—the same piercing blue as his son's—settled on me. "Lady Alora," he said, his voice carried through the hall. "Sunneva rejoices at your safe return."

I sank into a deep curtsy, keeping my eyes lowered. "Your Majesty. I am grateful to be home."

The lie tasted bitter on my tongue, but was delivered perfectly nonetheless.

"Come," the king said as he rose from his throne. "We have much to discuss. In private."

The crowd murmured as the king led us through a side door and into his private study. Guards stationed themselves outside, but

Kyler followed without a second thought. The prince's second was held above the rest.

Once the door closed, the king's warm facade cooled considerably.

"So," he said, circling me like a predator. "You've had quite the adventure, haven't you?"

I kept my posture straight, my expression neutral. "Not by choice, Your Majesty."

His eyes narrowed. "No? And yet you return with my son's guard." He glanced at Kyler, who stood silently by the door. "Curious company for a kidnapping victim."

"Kyler was instrumental in her rescue," Ryn interjected smoothly. "He found the trail that led to her safe return. We owe him a debt of gratitude."

The king hummed, unconvinced. "And what exactly did you discover during this... rescue? What of the ones who orchestrated such a breach? You are ultimately in charge of the prince's, and therefore the princess consort's, safety, are you not?" The king's gaze bore into Kyler. To my mates' credit, if he was affected at all by the ruler's pointed questions, he didn't show it.

"That is why I chose to deploy him, Father." Oryn's hand found mine, gently lacing his fingers with my own. "He's paid his penance and will not fail me again in protecting my wife. As for who did this, there is still an active investigation. We suspect bandits from the eastern lands beyond our waters."

The king's gaze lingered on our joined hands before shifting back to my face. "Is that so? Did you come to know your captures?"

I shook my head solemnly. "My eyes were bound the entire time until Sir Kyler found me. I only heard whispers of their plans to return to their ship."

After what felt like an eternity of scrutiny, the king finally nodded. "I'm sure you wish to rest before tonight's feast." He turned to Ryn. "Son, a word."

The door behind us creaked open. Magnus materialized at my side, his familiar presence a genuine comfort in this den of vipers. Kyler caught my eye briefly as I turned to leave, his face impassive but his concern flowed through our bond.

"This way, my lady," Magnus said, offering his arm.

As we walked through the corridors, the weight of the palace pressing down on me was apparent once more.

My shoulders began to ache with every step. The stress of performing a convincing act for the king exhausted me more than I thought it would. I spent my whole life pretending. Pretending I wasn't in love with Maël when it felt like his heart was elsewhere, every persona I adopted to carry out my orders, being Oryn's blushing bride while secretly hunting Johan and planning to leave before we made it to the altar. Different masks with different purposes, shed like a second skin when no longer needed.

"It's good to see you, Magnus," I said quietly, keeping my voice low enough that only he could hear.

His weathered face softened. "The feeling is mutual, my lady." Regret shone in his eyes as he peered down at me. "It was my own failures that allowed this to happen. I feared I might never see you again. I will not fail you again, Lady Alora."

"I'm harder to kill than that," I said with a small smile. "Don't fret over it too much. I don't blame you for the actions of corrupted men."

Magnus chuckled, but his eyes remained serious. "I have no doubt you are a force when the need arises. You'll need it. Court has changed in your absence."

I glanced up at him, the thoughts of Oryn being behind everything instantly crept into my mind. Is that why his father kept him there? But Kyler also stayed, didn't he? Was I fooled once again?

Unable to take the thought a second more, I reached out to him.

Are you still with the king and Ryn?

I am. Is everything okay? Do you need me? Concern hung heavy in his voice.

No, I said, *just feeling a little left out and in the dark.*

A hum resounded through the bond before a picture played in my mind like it was like a memory. I watched the king question Oryn further, discussing the loss at Souoak because he and Kyler were not there to lead the troops as they should have been, along with more military strategy.

As quickly as it appeared, it left, leaving me once again strolling the quiet halls with my stoic guard.

What was that? How did you do that?

I learned it from you. I wasn't sure I was doing it right, but I'm not in a position to do more at the moment. It was our conversation from moments ago.

From me? I've never done that. I shook my head, partly hoping I was just hallucinating for a moment.

"Are you feeling well, Lady Alora?" Magnus asked, his brow quirked in my direction.

I patted his arm. "I'm just tired," I assured.

What do you mean you learned that from me?

Hesitation came through our connection before Kyler's words. *You share things in your sleep.*

Share things? What kinds of things?

Nightmares, Lor. At first I wasn't sure and thought they were your dreams until I saw that night. I lived it through you. I was able to connect what I saw nights prior to what you told me before. I should have told you sooner, but I... I wasn't sure how to without causing you distress. Rasher is usually the one to handle sensitive matters.

Like this is any—I stopped myself before furthering my initial thought. The sting of being betrayed yet again faded as I considered each word carefully. Could I say without a doubt I could handle seeing his most traumatizing moments without warning? I knew all too well how awful his communication could be. Rasher may be large and deadly, but he mastered relationships more than anyone I knew. He always seemed to know what to say. Kyler didn't possess such a skill. The prince was more unrefined than one would think, unabashedly unafraid to say what was on his mind.

We'll talk about this later. I said, before bringing my attention back to Magnus and our silent walk. The door to Oryn's chambers was now before us.

He bowed slightly. "I'll be outside if you need me."

I gave him a kind smile. "Thank you, Magnus."

When I pushed open the door, Luella stood in the center of the room, her hands clasped tightly at her waist. The moment she saw me, her composure crumbled.

"My lady!" she cried, rushing forward. Tears streamed down her face as she threw her arms around me. "You're alive! You're really alive!"

I hugged her back, surprised by how natural it felt to embrace the woman. She had been my only friend within these gilded walls.

"I am," I said, patting her back awkwardly. "It's good to see you too, Luella."

She pulled back, wiping her eyes. "I never gave up hope. Not once. Even when they started saying you might be dead."

"Well, as you can see, the rumors of my demise were greatly exaggerated."

Luella laughed through her tears, then immediately switched to her handmaiden duties. "The feast will begin in two hours. We must get you ready. I've drawn a bath, and I've laid out three gowns for you to choose from."

As she helped me undress and settle into the steaming water, Luella's chatter flowed non-stop.

"You wouldn't believe the things they've been saying! That you ran away, that you were kidnapped by Esmeranian spies, that you'd been taken and murdered!" She poured scented oil into the water. "And that awful Lady Ingrid has been strutting around the palace like she already wears the crown. The moment you disappeared, she attached herself to Prince Oryn like a leech."

I stiffened. "Did she now?"

"Oh yes! Followed him everywhere, trying to console him in his grief." Luella rolled her eyes. "As if she cared about anything but taking your place. The prince left quickly to search for you though—*gods*—how romantic is that to have a prince desperate to find you, refusing to stop until you're back in his arms?" A heavy sigh left her body. "Anyway, her father's been pushing for a match between them, claiming the kingdom needs stability."

"Did my husband agree?" I asked, trying to keep my voice casual despite the question's gravity.

Luella smiled triumphantly. "He refused outright. He knew you were alive and that he would find you."

Something twisted in my chest—guilt, perhaps, or the unwanted remnants of feelings I couldn't afford anymore. Even if my heart changed, I knew I had cut him deeply with my scheme. He may be willing to lie to keep our heads attached to our bodies, but that didn't mean he cared.

Luella continued gossiping as she helped me dress and arranged my hair in an elegant style. Dark braids twisted from my temple to their meeting point where they fell with the rest of my curled locks. I was only half-listening, my mind racing with what was next, with facing the nobles once again.

A knock at the door interrupted Luella's latest tale about one of the duke's being caught with one of the king's mistresses. She opened it, and Oryn stood in the doorway, still in his travel wear, his golden hair gleamed in the lamplight.

"May I escort my wife to dinner?" he asked, his eyes finding mine across the room.

CHAPTER 32

Luella cast a knowing look between us before dipping into a curtsy. "I'll leave you to prepare, Your Highness. My lady." She slipped out, closing the door behind her with a soft click.

Oryn stood there, still as stone, his jaw clenched tight. The silence between us stretched as taut as a bowstring.

"I need to change," he finally said, moving toward his wardrobe.

I turned away as he began unfastening his travel-worn clothes, and I focused intently on adjusting my emerald gown's sleeves. A whisper of fabric slid against skin, pulling at my attention. I bit my lip, fighting the urge to look over my shoulder at the man who'd once filled my stomach with butterflies.

"Ready?" his voice startled me.

I turned to find him dressed in formal attire—deep red and gold that emphasized the breadth of his shoulders and the lean strength of his body. Damn him for being so beautiful.

I nodded, accepting his offered arm.

He stopped just before opening the door. "Before we go," he turned to me as he took my hand, cradling it in his palm. His other hand disappeared into his pocket, pulling out a ring. "It was still being made when we got married, so I wasn't able to give it to you then."

As he gently slid it onto my finger, words stuck in my throat. The golden band gleamed, etched with swirling patterns until they met the glittering stone that perched in the center. It was far nicer than anything I had, and even more intricate than the silver ring that hung around my neck.

Meeting his eyes, I managed to say, "I didn't give you a ring. I can't accept this."

"I don't need a ring to know where my heart lies, but I can send for one for appearances." He threaded our arms once again before he reached for the door.

"For appearances," I said as the door opened, confusion from the moment clouded my thoughts. Did he mean he only gave it to me for appearances? I considered the alternative, Oryn would have no other reason to gift me something so extravagant.

We walked in silence through the palace corridors, our steps matched as if we'd had months of practice. Guards lined our path, their eyes following our every move.

"Remember," Oryn murmured as we approached the grand hall's entrance, "we're madly in love."

"How could I forget?" I whispered back, plastering on my most convincing smile, though I wasn't so sure who I was trying to convince anymore.

The herald announced our arrival, and all eyes turned toward us. "His Royal Highness Prince Oryn and Her Royal Highness Princess Consort Alora!"

The nobles of Sunneva's court parted like water as we descended the stairs. I recognized the predatory gleam in their eyes—the same look wolves gave when spotting wounded prey.

Lord Renwick approached first, his smile not reaching his eyes.

"Your Highness, what a blessed relief to have you returned safely to us."

"Indeed," added Lady Vora, her gaze sharp as she assessed me. "We've all been simply distraught. Tell us, where did these awful kidnappers take you?"

I felt Oryn's arm tense beneath my fingers.

"I'm afraid that's still a sensitive matter under investigation," I replied smoothly, "but I'm grateful for the kingdom's concern during my absence."

"Such loyalty from our prince," Lord Renwick continued, his eyes darting between us. "Many of the nobles wished for... alternative arrangements. Despite the pressure, he refused."

"My husband's devotion is unmatched," I said, squeezing Oryn's arm in warning.

As he led us to our seats toward the head of the table, I caught Kyler standing guard in the corner.

A musical laugh cut through the atmosphere. "There you are, Love!"

A woman with perfectly coiffed brown hair and a dress cut dangerously low glided toward us.

Ingrid.

I'd recognized that pinched face anywhere, though she'd tried to soften it with blush.

"Lady Ingrid," Oryn acknowledged stiffly.

She ignored me, placing her hand on his free arm. "I'm so glad you've finally returned. I was so lonely here without you. Save a dance for me?"

Anger rolled through me and it was all I could do to shove it down. The woman had no shame. Touching my mate, I wanted to cut off every piece of her that brushed against him.

"Of course," Oryn said, sending shockwaves through me.

"You don't mind, do you, Princess Alora?" Her tight smile did nothing to hide the intent behind her sickly sweet tone. "After all, your capture has brought us quite close. Like old friends naturally do."

"I'm sure you have," I said, meeting her gaze directly. "How fortunate my husband has such concerned friends."

I noticed a servant lingering nearby, watching our interaction with unusual intensity before slipping away to where the king sat at the head of the long table. Another servant across the room mirrored the action.

Ryn pulled my chair out and I took my seat, the scarlet velvet of the armrests catching my gown's sleeves.

Luella appeared at my side with a goblet of wine. "A drink, my lady?"

As I accepted it, she looked as if she had something else to say, but scurried away.

I tasted the wine, the usual rich red blend the king favored, scanning the crowd with practiced nonchalance. The nobles of Sunneva's court circled us like sharks, scenting blood in the water.

Lady Merith sat across from me, clearing her throat. Her silver-streaked hair piled atop her head in an elegant style that likely required three handmaidens to create. "Princess Alora, what a relief to see you safe!" Her words dripped with honey, but her eyes remained cold. "Though I must say, captivity seems to have... changed you."

"How so, Lady Merith?" I asked, tilting my head with feigned innocence.

"There's a certain... aura about you now." Her gaze flicked across my face, as if searching for visible proof that things were not as they appeared. "One might wonder what exactly happened during your time away."

"One might," I agreed pleasantly, "but I assure you, I remain quite the same."

Lord Darius sat beside me, his rotund figure barely contained by his formal attire. "Your Highness," he said, bowing his head towards

Ryn before addressing me. "The timing of your return is most... fortuitous."

"Is it?" I answered for Ryn, maintaining my smile.

"Indeed. With the recent unrest in our northern territories and whispers of Esmeray forces moving along our borders," he leaned closer, lowering his voice, "some might find it curious how you escaped your captors so... unscathed."

Oryn's hand tightened on mine. "Are you implying something, Lord Darius?"

The lord's jowls quivered as he laughed. "Merely an observation, Your Highness. After all, your bride is just as beautiful as your wedding day. Not a scratch or a blemish in sight."

Lady Callista slid into our conversation from her spot next to Lady Merith, her fan fluttered like a nervous bird. "I heard the most fascinating rumor, Princess. They say you ran off with your lover." Her eyes gleamed with malice. "Of course, I dismissed such nonsense immediately."

"How thoughtful of you," I replied, keeping my voice steady despite the rapid beating of my heart.

"Though it does make one wonder," she continued, "how a captive princess manages to elude her kidnappers who seemed to so easily steal her away from her chambers."

I felt Oryn's body tense beside me, ready to intervene, but I squeezed his fingers in warning. These snakes wanted a reaction—I wouldn't give them the satisfaction.

"Perhaps," I said with a slight smile, "I'm simply more resourceful than you would have been in such a situation, Lady Callista."

I sipped my wine, keeping my smile fixed in place, meeting the eyes of those around me. Charming masks hid conniving smiles. Unfortunately for them, I knew their type well. This game of snakes and spies had begun.

CHAPTER 33

I watched as Ingrid appeared at our table; her smile all teeth and no warmth. She extended a gloved hand toward Oryn, her eyes looking me over until she saw his hand holding mine on his thigh. Her eyes darkened, surely catching sight of his gift to me. Satisfaction coursed through me. Maybe it wasn't so bad accepting his ring.

"I believe you promised me a dance, Your Highness."

Oryn hesitated, his eyes flicking to me. "Perhaps later—"

"Nonsense," she interrupted, her fingers brushing his shoulder. "The musicians have just begun my favorite melody."

My stomach clenched as Oryn stood, offering a placating look my way. "Just one dance, Love."

"Of course," I said. The words might as well have been coated in poison.

Ingrid's triumphant smile burned into me as she led him away, her hand possessively curled around his arm. I watched them move to the center of the hall, where she pressed herself closer than propriety allowed. For every one of their gliding sweeps, my wine turned more bitter on my tongue.

I couldn't do this. Not tonight. Not when I was so conflicted with Oryn. Not with her hands all over him, her laughter carrying across the room as she gazed adoringly into his eyes. The performance was too much.

I rose abruptly, muttering an excuse about needing fresh air to no one in particular. They didn't try to stop me as I slipped away from the table, keeping to the shadows along the wall. The weight of watchful eyes followed me—making me doubt our story was fully believed.

The corridor outside the great hall offered momentary relief from the suffocating atmosphere. I walked quickly, no destination in mind beyond escape. Regardless of how well-known these halls seemed, they would always be unfamiliar. I was the outsider who didn't belong. The wolf in sheep's clothing.

A hand caught my wrist, pulling me into a darkened alcove hidden behind a heavy tapestry depicting some ancient Sunnevean victory. I pulled my other arm back, ready to swing before recognizing Kyler's scent.

"You shouldn't be here," I whispered, instantly melting into his arms.

"Neither should you," he murmured, his breath warm against my ear. "The king has increased the palace detail, and no doubt many of his spies lie waiting for information to trade for coin."

"I couldn't stay there another minute," my voice cracked, "watching her with him—"

His lips silenced mine, desperate and hungry. My back pressed against the cold stone wall as his hands found my waist, pulling me against him. I tangled my fingers in his hair, losing myself in his touch, in the sensation of him solid and real against me.

He pulled away, brushing a wisp of my hair that had fallen across my face. "It's alright to love him, Princess."

"Is it?" I asked. "All this time I thought he hurt me, played me, then I took another mate, tried to sever from him. He's hardly spoken to me."

"And yet," he lifted the hand where the new ring perched upon my finger, "he still gave you this."

I looked at the stone. Despite the darkness around us, it still seemed to keep its sparkle. "He said it was for appearances."

He hummed, unconvinced. "I always thought I only saw the worst in others," he said, "but there are so many dark thoughts in that pretty head of yours. It really puts my reputation to shame."

His hand slid up my side, fingers grazing the underside of my breast through my gown. I gasped, arching into his touch as his fingers rolled my nipples. Reaching down his muscular abdomen, my fingers brushed against his hardening length. He groaned as I continued to rub him, his fingers leaving my nipples. A whine escaped my throat until they found where the heat collected. A thick finger slid down between my folds as I gasped, melting into the pleasure of his touch. He entered me, one finger, then two.

"This dress would look beautiful torn across the floor. My jaw nearly dropped when you arrived. Do you know how hard it was to not snatch you away from him? To show them you belonged to me by claiming you on the table." He brought his fingers to his mouth, sucking my juices off. His eyes rolled into the back of his head for just a moment as he returned them, this time pumping with more intensity. "You're the best thing I have ever tasted."

As his fingers pressed against that spot inside me, I couldn't help the breathy moan that left my lips, his name on my tongue. It only spurred him on more as he captured my lips, swallowing the sounds he elicited from me as that wave of pleasure crashed through me and had me tightening around his digits.

Footsteps echoed in the corridor, growing louder. We froze, barely breathing. The rhythmic click of armor told us it was the royal guard.

Kyler pressed his forehead to mine as we listened to the guards pass by, mere inches from our hiding spot. Only when their footsteps faded did we exhale.

"They've changed the patrol patterns," he whispered, "I thought we had more time before they came this way."

"We need to be careful," I said, reluctantly putting space between us. "If we're caught—"

"We won't be." His eyes gleamed in the darkness. "We need to be smarter about it. Oryn wouldn't say anything. If it bothered him that much, he would've found us already. But if it were anyone else, you being found unfaithful would complicate things."

"Agreed." I straightened my gown, smoothing the wrinkles his hands had created. "What do you mean he would've found us?" I asked.

A soft chuckle escaped him as he straightened himself up. "I know you like to keep him out, but I doubt that stopped him from feeling the ecstasy that is your pleasure."

Oh god. "He can feel... that?"

Kyler shrugged. "It's just a theory. I've noticed slight reactions from him when you seem to be feeling intense emotions. I don't think you can ever really close the bond, not entirely. The connection is still there."

Lovely. All the effort I've put into keeping that door between us shut felt futile if he could still sense any emotion from me. I was only saving myself from his voice flooding my head.

With Kyler's help, I slipped back into the feast before anyone seemed to notice my absence. Or perhaps they merely didn't care. As I took my seat once again, Oryn returned from his dance with Ingrid. His eyes met mine questioningly, but I simply smiled and took a sip of wine, ignoring the flush I knew still colored my cheeks.

"You seem... refreshed," he murmured, taking his seat beside me. The scent of citrus flooded my senses, enticing me to lean closer for more of the heavenly scent. It was an act of a god that I didn't succumb to the temptation.

"The night air did me good," I replied, avoiding his gaze.

The rest of the evening dragged on endlessly, a parade of nobles offering false welcomes and probing questions. By the time we finally retired to our chambers, exhaustion had settled deep in my bones.

Oryn and I moved around each other like wary dancers, the tension between us thick enough to cut with my daggers. When we finally slipped beneath the sheets, he kept to his side of the bed, and I to mine—a vast, cold expanse between us.

Sleep came fitfully, my dreams haunted by Death's warnings and the weight of the choices I'd made.

Morning arrived, the harsh sunlight streaming through the windows. I blinked awake to find Oryn already gone, the impression of his body on the sheets was the only evidence he'd been there at all. A note rested on his pillow.

Council meeting. We'll speak later.

I SIGHED, pushing myself up. Today would be no easier than yesterday—navigating the treacherous waters of court while maintaining the facade of a princess. And somewhere in this palace, something sinister that threatened to consume us all was being hidden.

Luella arrived with breakfast and fresh clothes, her cheerful chatter a welcome distraction from my thoughts. As she helped me dress, I caught sight of my reflection in the mirror—the perfect image of a Sunnevean royal. The mask was firmly in place, but beneath it, my resolved hardened.

Whatever game the king was playing, whatever Ingrid schemed, whatever fate had in store—I would be ready.

CHAPTER 34

With Oryn, and therefore his father, disposed for the time being, I took advantage of the freedom by dragging Luella down to the royal library for a visit, just like we used to.

Only this time, I wasn't looking for romantic novels as an escape.

The royal library was something to behold, more than all the gold the king furnished his residence with. The main room was open and airy, tables set up near a large window looking out over the gardens. Around the window were floor to ceiling shelves of books, most of which I have yet to see. A spiral staircase led to a second-floor balcony overlooking those reading below. Well, that is, if someone wanted to watch a reader devour a book.

I always enjoyed watching you read, Maël said nonchalantly in my head. *I could always tell something bad happened by the way your brows came together. It looked like you had one long brow.*

That doesn't sound creepy, or insulting at all, I deadpanned.

His laugh filled the space. It felt like it had been so long since my mind had conjured the hallucination of him that I almost began to miss it, like I missed the real man.

Oh, I'm quite real. If only I weren't trapped in your head, then we could re-enact some of the books you've read.

Even when I'm going crazy, you still tease me.

It's a love language.

He receded once again as I stared at the overflowing shelves before me, determined to find something of use.

"Luella," I said. "Do you know where I could find the historical books?"

"Historical will be over here, my lady," she beckoned me to follow her as she steered us left towards the dusty shelving.

"It's just the two of us. Alora or Lor is just fine." I reminded her. Sunneva may have an abhorrent culture of looking down upon those that keep this castle running, but I saw Luella as my equal and refuse to treat her as anything less. I only went along with it while in company. Miss Gregoria was known to be quick to punish.

"Yes... Lor," she hesitated, as if breaking a cardinal rule. I wanted to laugh, but didn't want it to discourage the progress we were making.

I began with the basic histories, royal families, wars, and the different economic systems that have shaped Sunneva to be what it was today. Nothing I needed for now. It wasn't until I had almost walked through this entire half of the library that I found what I was looking for. Books that mentioned magic, prophecies, and the lost gods. I pulled several from the shelf, refusing Luella's frantic offers to help.

Hours passed as I poured over the ancient tomes, making mental notes of inconsistencies.

When I found a section that mentioned Chaos—a god just as powerful as Fate and Death, my fingers trembled. The texts had been altered—subtle changes in wording, with ink that didn't quite match. Someone had been rewriting history.

More disturbing were the books about prophecies. Most seemed silly and benign, but others spoke of much more sinister things, of gods ripping holes in the earth to unleash a horde of demons and sacrifices. Whole pages were ripped out, some soiled with black ink. I tried to look beyond the mess, but couldn't get a grasp of the words.

"My la—Alora?" Luella's voice startled me. "It's nearly time for dinner."

I closed the book I was examining. "Thank you. Would you help me prepare?"

She nodded as she gathered the books I'd strewn about, helping me place them back onto the shelves before stepping out of the quiet solitude.

Back in my chambers, as she arranged my hair, Luella leaned close. "There's something I feel you should be wary of," she whispered. "The king has been acting strangely."

My hands stilled. "How so?"

"He wanders the castle at night. The guards change shifts at odd hours—on the third bell instead of fourth. And one of the maids was cleaning near his study and heard him talking to someone," she continued, her voice barely audible. "But no one was in the room with him."

I met her eyes in the mirror. Perhaps the king had a secret entrance in the room. It would be practical in a time of need. Still, we needed to know what he was up to. "Can you find out more?"

She nodded. "The servants talk. I'm an excellent listener."

"You are, but be careful," I warned. "This isn't just court gossip. Don't risk your life. It's not worth it."

"I understand." Her fingers worked deftly through my hair. "Though I disagree, you are worth it, my lady. I am happy to serve you in whatever way you need."

It wasn't long before Oryn came to collect me once again. Magnus was more than capable of seeing me to my appointments, but whenever we're both in attendance, the prince has escorted me personally.

Tonight, we were to attend a formal court function side by side, the picture of royal harmony. *Of power*, as his father would put it. Oryn played his part flawlessly—attentive and respectful, the charming prince he had always been. Yet the space between us might as well have been an ocean. Part of me was relieved to see that side of him, maybe even gave me hope that he had been truthful, that he wasn't behind my capture. As much as things have changed, there would always be a piece of me wishing they could be different. Could he forgive me for pleading to Death to sever our bond?

Since our return, he was always gone before I awoke. Nothing but a note left with promises to talk later, but later never came. We silently went to bed, then did the same thing the next day. The truth hung unspoken between us.

The court dinner that followed was an exercise in restraint. Ingrid had somehow maneuvered herself to sit beside Oryn, while I was placed across from them—forced to observe as she leaned close, her hand casually resting on his arm. My hand casually rested above my hidden blade, just in case.

"You've been missed at the hunts, Your Highness," she purred, her fingers lingering on his sleeve.

Oryn smiled politely. "My duties have kept me occupied."

She laughed as though he'd said something incredibly witty. "Surely you can find time for pleasure among your duties."

My knife scraped against the plate as I cut my meat with more force than necessary. Oryn did nothing to discourage her advances— no shifting away, no removal of her hand from his arm. Not even a shameful look at me for being so forthright.

Something twisted painfully in my chest as I watched them. I knew our marriage was a facade now, knew I also had another who I had given part of my heart to, yet seeing him with Ingrid awakened an emotion I wasn't prepared for.

CHAPTER 35

I awoke to another empty bed, the sheets beside me cold. Another day holding this pattern of avoidance. Oryn and I circled each other like wary predators, maintaining our act for the court while barely exchanging words in private. What's worse was because Ryn was gone, Kyler was as well. I was always left to my own devices once again. Good thing I always worked best alone.

Today brought a new challenge—the royal council meeting. As princess consort, my attendance was expected, though my input would be largely ignored. I dressed carefully, choosing a gown that balanced the trending court fashions with practicality, sliding my dagger into my hidden sheath. I was surprised to find Magnus waiting to escort me instead of Oryn. My husband had been consistent in retrieving me himself for mutual appointments, but not today. Unease hung in the air around me, suffocating me with the eerie feeling that something was happening.

The council chamber buzzed with hushed conversations when I entered. Oryn was already seated at his father's right hand, the king's chair still empty. My designated place waited opposite of

Oryn, but what caught my attention was Ingrid. She stood by Oryn's chair rather than in her assigned seat as a representative of her house.

She leaned down, whispering something that made him nod thoughtfully. Her hand rested on his arm, fingers tracing small circles on his sleeve. I thought it was strange he didn't show up this morning, but now I knew I was an idiot for thinking he was tied up with tasks. No, he was tied up with *her*. Something dark and primal stirred within me, a possessive rage I had no claim to given my own divided heart.

The candles in the room flickered as shadows began to pool at my feet, stretching across the floor like spilled ink. I sensed the power rise unbidden, my control slipping as Ingrid's fingers continued their casual claiming of my husband.

"Lady Alora." Kyler's voice came from behind me, his hand briefly touching the small of my back. "There was a request for you to review these reports before the meeting begins."

He pressed papers into my hands, his eyes conveying a silent warning. I took a deep breath, forcing the shadows back, feeling them retreat reluctantly.

"Thank you," I murmured, grateful for his intervention.

Are you okay? He asked through the bond.

I would feel much better if I could flay the skin from her very bones, I answered.

Please refrain from maiming anyone in here. There are too many guards for me and Oryn to fight off by ourselves.

I don't think Oryn would be much help. I fought the urge to cut a sharp look toward the sun-blessed prince himself. No, if I wanted to remain calm, I needed to focus on anything but him.

I disagree.

The candles steadied as I took my seat, noticing curious glances from the council members who'd noticed the change in the air.

Kyler positioned himself against the wall behind me, his presence a comforting anchor as the king finally entered and the meeting began. Ingrid returned to her seat, but her eyes constantly drifted to Oryn, a calculating smile playing on her lips.

I focused on breathing evenly, on maintaining control. I couldn't afford to reveal my hand—or powers—before I understood what was transpiring in the dark.

The king called the council to order, and I straightened my spine, face composed with dignity. Let them underestimate me. Let them get too comfortable in thinking they held the power here. Kyler was wrong before. I didn't need him or Oryn to make it out of this room alive if the need arose. I was Death's Wraith, no one could survive me.

The council meeting droned on for what felt like eternity. Lords and ladies debated grain tariffs and border patrols while I feigned interest, my mind racing with plans. Once we were dismissed, I returned to my chambers. I had work to do.

I spent the rest of the afternoon in a daze, my mind churning with questions. The council meeting hadn't been helpful, not that I expected secrets to be spilt. The king's increase in guard, his late night rendezvous, a prophecy promising power, and a cackling witch whose ear belonged to Fate. Those were what I cared about. All pieces on a board I couldn't fully see.

After dinner—where I pushed food around my plate while enduring more of Ingrid's thinly veiled barbs—I retreated to my chambers. Luella helped me undress, chattering about court gossip while I nodded absently.

"Lady Alora, are you listening?" she asked, concern in her eyes.

"I'm sorry, Luella. I'm just a little tired." I squeezed her hand.

"You should get some rest." She said. Luella helped me into my bed while she hurried about finishing her duties before quietly closing the door behind her.

Once alone, I waited. The palace quieted as night deepened. Oryn had come to bed hours later, the soft rhythm of his breath was a sure sign he was asleep. I quickly slipped on my gear: black leathers, a dark shirt, and my old boots that I had found in my wardrobe. All of my daggers were strapped to me, just in case. If I were caught, I only needed to get myself out of here. I could meet up with Rasher and Lucas. Kyler would come to us once it was safe.

The guard rotation passed our door precisely when Magnus said it would, something he drilled into me once I returned. He said it was best I knew, though I don't think he considered how I would use the information. I counted the seconds, then blanketed myself in my shadows, my body melting into darkness as I stepped into the hall.

Moving through the palace this way was risky, but necessary. The king's study was heavily guarded, with two men stationed outside. I kept close to the wall, working through the best way to get by, when the heavy oak door suddenly creaked open. The king strutted out briskly, barking orders at the two men to lock the door and follow him. One of the guards stumbled after him while the other fumbled with thick keys until he secured the room before chasing after his partner and ruler.

I moved to the door, pulling out a hairpin that stayed tucked into my boot. I was never much of a thief until I met Lucas, but it became necessary to learn to pick a lock quickly and quietly to get to some of our targets. I jammed the pin into the hole and used a dagger to start working it until I heard a resounding click. I slipped through the door, letting it quietly close behind me.

Moonlight filtered through tall windows, illuminating a massive desk covered in maps and correspondence. I moved silently, checking drawers and cabinets, finding nothing but routine matters of state.

Disappointment settled in my chest. This risk had been for nothing.

As I turned to leave, my eyes caught on a small irregularity in the wood paneling behind the desk. It was just below the atrociously sized painting the king had of himself hung against the wall. Pressing my fingers against it revealed a hidden compartment. Inside lay a leather-bound journal, its pages littered with cramped handwriting.

My heart stuttered as I recognized the symbols drawn in the margins—alchemical notations like those that had been carved into my skin.

I flipped through pages of experimental records, my stomach churning at clinical descriptions of "the subject's" responses to various stimuli.

My responses.

My pain.

Then I found it—a letter tucked between pages.

Your Majesty,

The female subject's blood contains properties unlike anything I've encountered. When combined with the correct catalysts, it produces a reaction capable of enhancing magical abilities tenfold. It is my belief this is the prophecy's promise. If I can stabilize this into another host, we could enhance an army that would be unstoppable. She'll be most pleased.

I require more samples to complete my work. The current extraction methods are inefficient—combined with the suppressants, the subject weakens too quickly. I recommend more sustainable harvesting protocols to maximize yield without destroying the source.

Your obedient servant,
The Alchemist

My hands trembled as I read. I was no longer just a prisoner. I wasn't even considered a person. Just a source to be harvested from.

The sound of a key being slid into the lock caught my ear just as the doorknob turned with a soft click. I shoved the letter back into the journal, heart pounding as I slid it into the compartment. My fingers fumbled with the catch, precious seconds ticking away.

Heavy footsteps approached. The door creaked open.

I melted into shadow, pressing myself into the darkest corner as the king strode in, a lantern held high. His face was cast in harsh angles by the flickering light as he surveyed the room.

He moved to his desk first, checking the drawers I'd carefully shut. His eyes narrowed as he traced the edge of a paper I must have disturbed.

"Guards!" he barked.

The two men rushed in, weapons drawn. "Your Majesty?"

"Search the room. Someone's been here." He ran his fingers along the paneling where the hidden compartment lay.

The guards moved methodically through the space, checking behind curtains and under furniture. I stayed perfectly still, willing my racing heart to quiet. The tightening in my chest was a reminder not to move a muscle. One guard passed so close I could have touched him.

"Nothing, Your Majesty," the first guard reported. "No signs of forced entry."

The king's jaw clenched. "Go find the fools who were stationed here before and make sure their keys are on their person." His gaze swept the room once more, lingering for a heart-stopping moment on my hiding spot. "Someone was here. Find them."

The guards bowed and left. The king remained, studying the room with predatory focus. Finally, he extinguished his lantern and followed them out.

I waited until his footsteps faded before sliding out of the room. Only when I was safely back in my chambers, in my nightgown, and laying in the soft bed did I allow myself to breathe.

CHAPTER 36

I paced the length of my chambers. Dawn's first light broke through hours ago. Oryn had stepped out long ago while I pretended to still be asleep. Sleep had evaded me after what I'd discovered in the king's study. The letter burned in my mind—evidence that he'd authorized my torture, my imprisonment, all for some twisted magical experiment. It made me question everything that had happened since I stepped foot in the hall to do the assessment, when I first arrived. Aside from growing his army and the whispers I had managed to capture, it wasn't enough to cast suspicion on him for anything but what we already knew. The king sought power, accumulating it to drive his ambitions.

This, this changed everything. The king was playing a darker game and had found success through me, and now I was right back in his clutches.

I needed to tell Kyler. We needed to plan our next move before we fell into a trap. For a moment, I considered telling Oryn too. But where did his loyalties lie? With his father and crown, that was the logical choice.

It was now well into the afternoon; I tried contacting Kyler several times through our bond to arrange a meeting, but he was preoccupied with some last-minute orders. I didn't get much from him other than a 'we'll talk later' whenever that would be. I knew the castle's eyes had grown. As much as I knew he would come when I called, he wouldn't risk blowing our cover.

A soft knock at the door made me jump.

"My lady?" Luella's voice came through. "I've brought you tea."

I composed myself, smoothing my gown. "Come in."

Luella entered with a tray, her usual cheerful smile in place. "It's a new blend, it came all the way from the farthest desert city. They said the tea leaves sparkle in the sun."

"Wonderful," I lied, accepting the cup she offered. The warm porcelain felt grounding in my trembling hands.

"The court is buzzing about tonight's dinner," she said, moving to open the curtains. "All the nobles, even from the coastlines and desert, have arrived to attend. They hardly ever bother with the trip."

Perfect timing. A room full of witnesses would make it harder for the king to act against me openly.

"I was thinking you could wear the golden gown," Luella said, already moving to the wardrobe. "You'll look like the epitome of sun-blessed. I think we have some dusting we can brush on your skin to really make you shine."

"I'm not sure shining is really my thing," I said, allowing her to help me slip the dress on. The silk felt cool as it slunk to the floor. A slit exposed my leg almost to my hip. Thin straps held the plunging top up. A shiver crept up my spine at the exposure until a sense of thrill replaced it. The looks on my mate's faces would be priceless, at least one of them. Oryn would probably hold the same disinterested expression while we're alone and then pretend we are still happy once we have an audience. Kyler, on the other hand... I let a slight chuckle escape my throat. He would probably spend the night in my head demanding me to go change. This slip of a dress would ruin him while he can't openly touch me.

"Prince Oryn told Magnus he'd escort you personally. Let's get you finished up before he arrives to collect you." Luella finished brushing out my long hair, she chose to leave it down in loose curls, and turned to grab a canister and brush.

"Tilt your face up. You don't want to look like you just ate the treasury," she quipped. I followed her demands and tilted my face away from her workspace. She opened the jar. Fluffy glittering powder shifted with the lift of the lid, throwing tiny flecks into the air. She dipped her brush into it, lightly tapping along the side to remove the excess before light sweeps touched my shoulders. Luella painted the very tops of my arms and collarbone with the fine dust, careful not to let it settle anywhere else. The light brushes were tranquil, bringing peace as I closed my eyes and let her turn me into her masterpiece.

The soft thud of steps brought me back to the moment. Luella had stepped back, assessing her work.

"Perfect," she nodded to herself as she placed her tools down. "A princess made of gold."

I turned to the mirror, her words ringing true. She helped me into intricate shoes, gleaming like the dress. I looked like I was made of gold, like I had stepped out of the palace walls itself. The powder against my pale skin reminded me of stars as it trailed from one shoulder to the next. The shine was enhanced by the backdrop of my dark hair.

Luella fretted over a few curls behind my head as the heavy door creaked open. Oryn strode in, but stopped once his eyes fell on me. The air stilled as we stood in the stalemate. Two mates who fell out of love. The sharp stab of loss assaulted my heart. If things had been different, I could've loved this man for the rest of my life. He would have been the sunshine that lit my dark nights.

He broke the moment with a choked cough as he turned to his wardrobe for his clothes. He brushed past us to the en suite, only returning dressed in his formal wear. Rich crimsons and bright golds decorated his uniform, the golden sword strapped to his side was encrusted with a ruby hilt. The brilliant crown placed upon his head brought out the shimmering blue of his eyes. Handsome never really began to cover what he was, more god-like than a prince.

He held a thin golden tiara in his hand as he approached me, placing it on my head with a gentle hand. His eyes trailed along my face as I met his gaze, his hand lightly brushing down my cheek. I thought for a moment he would say something, maybe even compliment me, but he cleared his throat as he nodded towards the door.

"They're expecting us," he said, offering his arm.

I walked beside Oryn, my arm linked with his as he led us through the halls. No words were exchanged, not even so much as a cough or a hum as we entered the grand dining hall. The chandeliers sparkled overhead, casting golden light across the sea of nobles and dignitaries. My gown glinted in the light, making me appear every bit the princess consort I was supposed to be.

"Smile," Oryn whispered, his breath against my ear. "Everyone is watching."

I plastered on my most convincing smile as we took our seats at the high table. The king sat at the center, Oryn to his right, and me beside my husband. Across from us sat the ambassadors from the southeastern coast. The string wound around my heart pulled taunt. Kyler must be mere steps from me, because I could feel his familiar presence, a silent sentinel amidst the chattering dignitaries.

You look like a goddess. His deep voice filtered into my mind, a husky note proving my earlier hopes were becoming true.

If only I had someone to worship me later, I teased.

A growl rumbled between us. *I will pray at your altar all night if that is your wish.*

I wanted to preen at his words, but I knew the moment he got me alone we'd need to discuss more important things.

A servant filled my goblet with deep red wine. As I reached for it, something caught my eye—a faint shimmer around the rim, almost imperceptible in the candlelight. My fingers froze in midair.

"Is something wrong?" Oryn asked, his voice low but tense.

"Not at all," I replied, letting my hand fall back onto my lap. "Just admiring the craftsmanship of the goblets."

He quirked a brow. Honestly, I wouldn't have believed me either. I mentally ran through all the potentials: was the wine poisoned, or just the rim of the goblet? And very few poisons had a sheen like this. Vanya trained us to build up somewhat of an immunity to them, but I wasn't impervious, nor did I want to put myself in harm's way to save face. I couldn't alert Kyler right now without triggering a reaction, and if he knew I willingly drank the poison, I would never hear the end of it.

The first course arrived—a delicate soup of wild mushrooms. I pretended to sip my wine, bringing the goblet to my lips without letting the cup touch them.

Lady Callista sat to my right. She had never hid her disdain for me since my arrival. She turned away to speak with her other neighbor, giving me the opportunity I needed.

"Oh!" I exclaimed softly, knocking into her arm as I reached for a roll. "My apologies, Lady Callista."

In the momentary confusion, I switched our goblets, setting hers where mine had been.

"Do be more careful, Princess," she sniffed, turning back to her conversation.

I watched from the corner of my eye as she took a deep drink from what had been my goblet. Guilt twisted in my stomach, but I needed to know if my suspicions were correct. The best scenario— she would make it to a healer in time—the worst, she'd die.

The king rose to make a toast, and everyone lifted their glasses. I pretended to drink from Lady Callista's cup. It didn't have the same sheen around the rim, but I wouldn't take the chance.

Halfway through the main course, Lady Callista began to cough.

Her face flushed red, then drained to an alarming pallor. She clutched at her throat, eyes wide with panic.

"Help!" someone called, "Lady Callista needs a physician!"

Down the table, I caught Ingrid's face—not concerned, but frustrated. Her eyes darted to my stolen goblet, then to me. When our gazes met, her expression shifted to a practiced mask of worry. But I'd seen enough.

Ingrid had tried to poison me, and she severely underestimated her opponent.

The court physician rushed to her side, barking orders for various remedies. The hall buzzed with whispers, nobles leaning toward each other behind cupped hands. I kept my face carefully neutral as they carried Lady Callista from the hall, her body convulsing as the poison took hold.

"How dreadful," I murmured, setting down my untouched goblet.

The king rose from his seat, commanding attention. "Please, let us not allow this unfortunate incident to spoil our evening. Lady Callista is receiving the finest care. Pity she found herself allergic to such finery served tonight. Let us enjoy the night!"

Servants hurried to clear away the dishes, replacing the cups with fresh ones. New wine was poured. The musicians, who had fallen silent during the commotion, began to play again.

I felt Oryn's eyes on me. "You seem remarkably composed," he whispered.

"Should I not be, Prince Oryn?" I asked, cutting into my venison with precise movements.

"Most would be shaken by witnessing a poisoning."

"Most are not me." I met his gaze, holding the knife up slightly enough for it to catch his attention. "As I'm sure you are now aware. Good thing the physician was near, surely she'll be fine."

His brow furrowed, but before he pressed further, the king called for dancing to begin. The tables were cleared to the sides of the hall, creating space for couples to gather.

Ingrid appeared almost instantly at Oryn's side, her red silk gossamer gown shimmering in the candlelight. "Prince Oryn, would you honor me with a dance?" Her smile was sharp, like a cat ready to pounce on a mouse.

I turned away, pretending to be engrossed in conversations with the governor from Bridgedale. From the corner of my eye, I saw Oryn hesitate, glancing my way.

When I offered no reaction, he took Ingrid's hand. "Of course, Lady Ingrid."

They moved to the center of the floor. Her body pressed closer to his than should even be allowed. She laughed at something he said, touching his chest with her palm. The sight of her hands on him made my blood boil. Shadows curled along the edges of my skirt.

I forced myself to breathe, to appear indifferent. Let him have her if that's what he wanted. The gods knew he no longer wanted me.

But the thought of him wanting her twisted something painful inside me. Was this jealousy or wounded pride? I told myself it was merely the latter—the humiliation of being so publicly set aside by my husband while the court watched and whispered. I could even blame the bond itself. Surely that had its own effect.

I was contemplating an escape to the terrace when a hush fell over the crowd. The king had risen from his seat, his eyes fixed on me with predatory intent. My stomach knotted as he approached, bowing with exaggerated formality.

"Princess Alora, would you honor me with a dance?" His voice carried across the hall, ensuring everyone had heard.

Refusing wasn't an option. I forced a smile and curtsy before I placed my hand in his. "The honor is mine, Your Majesty."

The musicians began a slow, stately tune as he led me to the center of the floor. His hand pressed against the small of my back, fingers digging in just enough to remind me of his power.

"You've settled back into court life remarkably well," he said, guiding me through the steps. "One would hardly know you'd been through such an ordeal."

"My uncle ensured I had thorough lessons in adaptability, Your Majesty."

His laugh was bitter. "Indeed. Though I wonder if you truly understand what's expected of you now."

Over his shoulder, I spotted Oryn and Ingrid, still dancing. Her head rested on his chest, her eyes closed in apparent bliss. My shadows coiled beneath my skin, begging to be released as I forced it down.

"Great changes are coming to Sunneva," the king continued, his voice dropping to ensure only I could hear. "The old ways are fading. New power will rise."

I kept my expression neutral despite the chill his words sent through me. "Change is the nature of all things."

"Some resist it." His grip tightened. "The tide will sweep away those who refuse to accept it."

My gaze found Kyler, standing at attention against the wall. His face was a perfect guard's mask, but I saw the tension in his jaw, the slight flare of his nostrils. He couldn't intervene, couldn't save me from this dance or the king's veiled threats.

"A new age may just be what the people need," I said carefully.

I risked another glance at Oryn, now whispering something in Ingrid's ear that made her giggle. The sight burned, even as I told myself it shouldn't matter.

"Indeed," the king murmured, "I look forward to your utmost cooperation."

When the dance ended, I noticed them slip away together. Without thinking, I followed, keeping to the shadows as they wandered into the palace gardens. The night air was cool against my heated skin as I crept behind hedgerows, close enough to hear their voices.

"—never been a love match," Ingrid said, her voice soft and sympathetic. "everyone knows it was arranged for political reasons."

"My marriage is not a topic for discussion," Oryn replied, though his tone lacked conviction.

"But surely you've considered better matches?" She stepped closer to him. "Someone who understands court life, someone raised for this purpose."

"Lady Ingrid—"

"Someone who would never embarrass you by disappearing for months, only to return with your guard and strange stories." Her voice dropped lower. "Someone who could be discreet, who could give you comfort without demands."

I dug my nails into my palms, fighting to keep my shadows contained as rage built inside me.

"I could be that for you," Ingrid whispered. "No one has to know. I could warm your bed in a way she never could. Give you an heir with a better bloodline."

Before Oryn could answer, she pressed herself against him, capturing his lips with hers. I waited for him to push her away, to reject her advances.

One heartbeat. Two. Three.

His hands remained at his sides, neither embracing her nor pushing her away. I'd seen enough. I turned and fled through the gardens, shadows trailing from my fingertips like smoke. By the time I reached our chambers, my control was slipping. The darkness within me churned, responding to my fury, threatening to spill out and consume everything in its path.

CHAPTER 37

The darkness stormed inside me. How dare he? How dare she? Humiliation coursed through my veins. The memory of Ingrid's lips on Oryn's and his damn hesitation sent another wave of shadows spilling from my skin.

A vase shattered across the room without me touching it. I needed to get myself under control before I destroyed everything.

I stumbled to the bathing chamber, fumbling with the taps until steaming water began filling the large marble tub. My reflection caught my eye—violet eyes nearly white with power, shadows dancing across my skin like living tattoos. I barely recognized myself.

Stripping off my gown, I sank into the scalding water, hissing as it burned my skin. The pain helped ground me, forcing my focus away from the shadows and onto something tangible. I closed my eyes, willing my breathing to slow.

But the images wouldn't stop. Ingrid's hands on Oryn's chest. His lack of resistance. Their bodies pressed together while I stood watching like some pathetic, forgotten thing.

"I should have said something," I whispered to the empty room, tears slid down my cheeks. I kept replaying that moment when

Ingrid came to fetch him. He had looked at me, his eyes asking the question I was too stubborn to consider. I had no one to blame but myself.

At first our marriage had been arranged, but at some point I'd believed it could be more. That dream was ripped away from me, but what if he was innocent? The papers I found in his father's study never mentioned any involvement on his part. I considered every moment he had denied playing a part in it, every time I made him out to be the monster, each instance where I blew his words to the wind, away from the narrative I had clung to.

I was the undoing of us. He was never upset over being dragged with us, other than being chained. He had saved me. But I destroyed his love the moment I begged Death to separate us. Any semblance of being able to recover us had been destroyed by my own hand.

The water rippled as my power seeped from my fingertips, darkening it until it looked like the night sky. This was exactly what the noblewoman wanted—to drive me further away from him, to prove I didn't belong. And here I was, giving her exactly what she wanted.

The door crashed open, and Oryn stormed in, his jacket noticeably gone, leaving only a thin undershirt with the sleeves rolled up to his elbows. Anger permeated the surrounding air. Despite keeping the bond closed, I could still feel the emotion rolling off of him as he approached me.

I closed my eyes as I leaned my head back, giving myself one last moment to collect myself before facing him. "Give me a few more minutes. I'll be gone so you and your mistress can have your bed for the night. I'll go to my old rooms." My voice cracked more than I cared to admit, but soon I would be out of his way. I did enough damage. I should just step aside and let him have his happiness.

"You're not going anywhere, Love. Not until you tell me why you left without me, and why you seem to think I have a mistress when my heart belongs solely to you."

I laughed, opening my eyes to look him in the eye. "You say your heart belongs to me, yet you've done nothing but shower Ingrid in your affections. That kiss in the garden was really sweet. Stolen moments in the night are *so* romantic."

"That's not what happened," his eyes flashed, "if you would've hung around you would've known as much."

I hummed in thought. "And watch the two of you make a fool out of me? No thank you, I know when to take my leave."

He sighed, running a hand through his hair. "She kissed me, I was caught off guard."

"You didn't push her away. You never push her away."

"I was about to until becoming distracted by the utter anguish I felt coming through our bond," his voice rose, "You didn't even give me a chance to handle it before you ran off."

"Handle it?" I stood up, water cascading off me, not caring about my nakedness. "Like you've handled everything else?"

His jaw clenched. "I've told you, I had nothing to do with that."

"I know," I cried. Giant tears fell from my eyes. "I didn't know until it was too late."

His hands clenched into tight fists as he stood there, bearing witness to my vulnerability.

"You knew and continued to keep me at arm's length?"

"You were too busy with court and Ingrid and whatever else was more important than your *wife*." The words burned my throat, but I couldn't stop my feelings from pouring out. "Don't pretend you haven't hated me since Runerth. I broke us while holding onto the idea you betrayed me." My voice grew quieter. "In the end, I betrayed you." I said, barely audible.

"You continued to punish me over Ingrid?" He demanded. "I only humored her advances because of the jealous rage I felt from you. Forgive me for taking the only shred of desire and attention you gave me since I saw you in Saints Landing. You're right Lor, you did betray me, but not for what you think."

We stared at each other, the air between us heavy with pain and accusations.

"I never wanted any of this," I whispered.

His eyes softened. "What you asked the gods for hurt, but I'm still here. Every day I leave before you rise, so I don't chase you off by begging you to forgive me. I can't stay away."

"I'm not sure I can let go that easily. Oryn, they *tortured* me. I laid on the floor of that grimy cell hoping it was all a cruel joke and you'd come to save me. You never came."

"I will always come, Alora. I will fight to get to you with my dying breath. Every night, I've been haunted with worry wondering where you were. Once we reunited, those nightmares turned to how could I have let that happen. If I knew, if I had any idea that's what you were enduring, I wouldn't have wasted any time in getting to you." His finger traced lightly along my shoulder. "All I'm asking is a chance to make things right, to prove to you that I can be the husband you deserve. Even if you can't forgive me fully right now, just let me try, Love. I'm ready to be everything that you need, I was ready the moment I met you in that godforsaken bar."

I thought about Jones's worn tavern, just as weary as it's clientele. "How can you say that when I—" I choked on the words, unable to voice what I had begged for on the misty island.

"Shh," his hand cupped my face, "I can say it because I've already forgiven you for that. I understand after what happened how you could've come to wanting to be severed from me. As much as the thought absolutely destroys me, I won't hold that moment in time against you."

"You'd forgive what I'd done? Just like that?" I questioned.

"There's very little I *wouldn't* forgive you for, Lor." He took a tentative step closer to me, taking my hands gently in his own. "I failed to protect you before, that I am guilty of, but I will never let you face danger alone. I will protect you, my wife, my mate. If you can forgive me for my negligence, if we can move forward, I can consider our time with Death a very bad dream."

"I think I can do that." A sob threatened to release itself, but I held it back, causing a cough to come out. I didn't realize how badly I needed for us to begin repairing the chasm that had been built between us.

"If we're going to survive what's coming, we need honesty between us."

I nodded slowly. "You're right." Taking a deep breath, I continued on. "If I'm going to forgive some of what's happened, you need to accept something, too." I met his gaze. "You can't hold it against Kyler that we also have a mate bond. He couldn't help it any more than we could. He's saved me several times. Doesn't that count for something?"

Oryn's eyes darkened as they raked over my naked form, the water glistening on my skin in the candlelight. The tension between us shifted, morphing from anger into something else entirely.

"You and Kyler," he said, his voice low and dangerous. "Do you know how much you've tortured me every time I could feel the ecstasy from you, knowing it was from his hands and not my own?"

I lifted my chin defiantly. "I—"

In one fluid motion, his hands gripped my waist and he lifted me from the tub. Water cascaded down my body, soaking the front of his shirt as he pressed me against him.

"And did you think of me while he touched you?" Oryn growled against my ear, sending shivers down my spine.

"No," I lied, my breath catching as his lips brushed my neck.

He carried me to the bed, tossing me onto the silken sheets without caring to dry me off. I propped back on my elbows, watching as he pulled his shirt off, revealing the sun that emblazoned the toned planes of his chest.

"Liar," he whispered, crawling over me like a predator. "I felt you,

Alora. Every time. I felt you reaching for our bond even as you tried to shut me out. Whether you meant to or not, you called to me."

My heart hammered against my ribs as he hovered above me, his eyes burning with possession and hurt. I wanted to deny it, to push him away, but my body betrayed me, arching toward him.

"You're my wife," he said, his fingers tracing the curve of my hip. "My mate. No matter who else claims a piece of your soul. You. Are. Mine."

His mouth crashed down on mine, hungry and demanding. I responded with equal fervor, my nails raking down his back as I pulled him closer. This wasn't forgiveness—this was a desperate attempt to reclaim what was once his.

"Tell me you want this," he commanded against my lips, his hand sliding between my thighs.

I gasped as his fingers found my entrance. "I do. I want this," I admitted. "I want you, Ryn."

With a growl, his fingers pressed further in. First one, then two. It was when he slid a third in that I began panting. His touch was as merciless as the kisses he claimed my mouth with. He began trailing his lips down my neck, sporadically biting as I tightened around his fingers. My vision began to go black.

"Let go, Lor. I've got you," he said, his voice hoarse as he moved further down to suck a nipple into his mouth. He teased the pebbled bud once he released it, circling it with the tip of his tongue.

I whined at the effect of his words, my body following his command and pleasure erupting inside of me. His fingers wrung every bit of it out from me until my body's convulsions finally subsided.

He finally removed himself from me, my core already missing the fullness. A smirk painted the golden prince's face as he continued to explore my body with his mouth. He licked his way down to the apex of my thighs, settling himself between them.

Torturous.

That's the only way to describe the feeling when he licked right up my center and took the most sensitive part of me in his mouth. He lifted his gaze up with a groan, nothing but adoration in his eyes.

"You don't know how badly I've been dying for a taste of you." He said as he bent back down to get his fill. As the pressure began to build once again, I threaded my hands into his thick blonde hair, the golden strands so soft to the touch.

I'm about to let go once again, but I need more, more of him. I tugged on his hair, bringing his face up.

"Oryn," I pant.

"Wife," he answered.

I huffed with annoyance. "Don't make me beg."

He sat up on his knees. My legs had no choice but to spread even further to accommodate him. His rigid cock proudly flexed as he brought a large hand to it, slowly stroking it while maintaining eye contact. The look in his eyes was clear that he's not budging until I give him what he wanted.

"Please, Ryn," I said.

"Please Ryn, *what?*"

This infuriating prince. I was tempted to kick him off and try to reach Kyler. But then again, my other mate would also like to make me beg for him. Damn the fates.

"Oryn," I tried to keep my tone sweet, but my words came out more carefully. "Please, I need you."

It's like any control left in him snapped. One moment he was on his knees, the next his weight settled upon me, one hand cradled my neck while the other gripped my hip. In one swift motion, he sheathed himself inside me. Our bond practically sang with the connection as he began rutting inside me. I thought he was desperate before, but his pupils had blown wide and each thrust became deeper and harder. I wrapped my arms around his neck, pulling him closer as I kissed his chest and neck. His hold was iron tight, bruising even. I took the pain in stride as I started barreling closer and closer to the edge. My poor mate has needed this, has needed *me* when all I did was turn him away. This punishing pace only heightened the pleasure that twisted in my core.

"Oryn," I gasped.

"Gods, you feel too damn good," he panted, "Fuck, be a good girl and fall with me, Love."

As if he had the power to demand such things, our bodies crashed together a few more times before we were both sent into oblivion. My name was a prayer on his lips as our pace slowed, his arms cradling me as we settled back into reality.

CHAPTER 38

I laid curled against Oryn's chest, our breathing finally slowed in tandem. His fingers traced lazy patterns along my spine, sending pleasant shivers through my still sensitive body.

"I've missed you," he murmured against my hair. "You've tortured me every moment of every day by being so close but out of my reach."

I tilted my face up to his, studying the softness in his eyes that I hadn't seen in so long. "I've missed parts of you, too."

His lips quirked. "Only parts?"

"The parts that aren't infuriating," I replied, but there was no heat in my words.

A sharp knock interrupted us before Oryn could respond. We both tensed, exchanging questioning glances. I opened the door from my mind to his, no longer needing to escape from him.

If that's Ingrid, I will kill her. I sent to him with a serious look in my eye.

They'll leave in a moment. He assured.

Mind opening the door for me, Princess? Kyler's voice filled the space.

Oryn groaned at hearing his voice, but did nothing to stop me as I rose from our bed to open the door. Kyler's eyes widened as I let him in, not a stitch of clothing on me.

I stood there, unashamed, letting the soft firelight caress my bare skin. Let them both get their fill. After all, they were mine as much as I was theirs. The marks Oryn had left on my body were a testament to that claim, and the hunger in Kyler's eyes as he took in the sight of me only confirmed it.

"Are you insane?" He demanded as he quickly stepped into the room and shut the door. "Someone could've seen you!"

"It was only you there," I shrugged.

"He's not wrong, Love." Oryn sat up against the headboard. "I'd be forced to banish anyone who saw you."

I rolled my eyes as I perched on the small sofa near the stone fireplace. "You two are ridiculous. You don't need to banish someone for accidentally seeing me when it's my own fault."

"The alternative is we remove their eyes," Kyler's jaw clenched as he took the spot beside me, a bottle of amber liquid clutched in his hand. The tension in the room shifted as Kyler's fingers ghosted across my shoulder, leaving a trail of icy sparks in their wake. I couldn't help but arch into his touch, even as Oryn's eyes darkened from his position on the bed. The air grew thick with unspoken desire, a dangerous dance of possession and need.

Oryn's fingers clenched around the sheets, his skin still gleamed with sweat from our earlier activities. His gaze never left us as Kyler's hand slid down my arm, possessive yet questioning. The bond wove tight around the three of us, destined to forever be bound.

"Certainly a fitting alternative," Oryn agreed as he rose from the bed and took to the armchair in front of us. The possessiveness of both men burned through their every movement, their territorial instincts radiated like waves of heat and ice. Oryn's fingers whitened against the armrests, his eyes tracking every breath, every subtle shift of my body, while Kyler's presence beside me was a predatory chill that made my skin prickle with awareness.

The air in the room crackled with unspoken tension, the scent of sex and sweat still lingered in the air. Moonlight filtered through the gauzy curtains, casting long shadows across the ornate furniture. The embers in the fireplace painted everything in a soft amber glow, matching the liquor in the bottle that passed between us.

I settled onto the plush velvet of the sofa, my bare skin prickling with goosebumps from both the cool air and the heated gazes of my mates.

"You called me a murderer," I met Kyler's eyes, "yet here you are, ready to maim someone?"

He popped the top off the bottle and took a long pull, his shoulders lifting in a casual shrug.

"The world is a brutal place, Princess. Especially when it comes to protecting what's mine," Kyler's voice was low and deadly, sending a shiver down my spine.

"Ours," Oryn corrected as he leaned down and swiped the bottle from his friend. "What brings you to our door, Kyler?" He drank deeply before passing the bottle to me.

The liquid scorched a path down my throat, its spice fierce enough to make my eyes water. I welcomed the burn, using it to ground myself between these two powerful fae males whose very presence seemed to electrify the air around us.

"Thought we could all use a drink after what your mistress has been spewing downstairs."

Oryn's expression turned lethal. "She's *not* my mistress."

Swallowing back the bitter taste of rage, I refused to let her lies poison this moment. "I assumed you were here because—" I gestured towards Oryn.

Kyler took another sip of the alcohol before setting it down. "I almost did until I realized your fear and anger weren't laced with pain. You were safe, and then... well, I could tell you two were making up. Honestly, I'm grateful." He fixed narrowed eyes on Oryn. "But that's not going to stop Ingrid."

"She's bold," I said, claiming the bottle and letting liquid fire chase away my darkening thoughts. "She made a pathetic attempt to poison me at dinner."

The air in the room felt like it was sucked out, both my mates went deadly still at my words.

"Come again?" The tone in Oryn's voice dropped to a deadly whisper, promising violence.

Kyler's gaze remained fixed on me as I looked from one to the other before letting out a sigh. "During dinner, my cup seemed off. The guild trained us to detect even the subtlest poisons. I had a hunch and I was right." I explained.

"If the poison was meant for you, how did Lady Callista fall ill?" Kyler demanded, his voice sharp.

Heat crept up my neck, staining my cheeks. "I switched our cups," I admitted, "but I recognized the poison. It wasn't lethal. I'm not sure Ingrid knew that, I caught her eye during the panic and she didn't seem pleased that I wasn't foaming at the mouth on the floor."

"Alora," Kyler sighed, raking his fingers through his hair. "Why are you just now telling us?"

"And what exactly would you two have done with that information?" I countered, lifting my chin.

"She'd be rotting in the ground by now," Oryn replied, his voice carrying the weight of a promise.

"Precisely," Kyler growled, a predatory gleam in his eyes. "I would have ended her right there. Instead, she's poisoning the court against you, spreading lies about your jealousy over the prince. Even worse, she's twisted the truth about Lady Callista."

"She'll be easy to handle." I assured.

I lifted the bottle to my lips, the fire spirit burning a path down my throat. The silence between Kyler and Oryn hung heavy as storm clouds, crackling with unspoken tension.

"We should talk about this," I said, my hand sweeping through the air between us.

Kyler's gaze locked onto mine, dark as midnight. "What exactly requires discussion? The fact that you two slipped away together?"

"That's not quite what I meant," I said.

"You could've joined us," Oryn purred, his golden smile returning. "Our mate clearly requires both of us to satisfy her needs."

I took control of the conversation back. There were more important things to discuss. "I meant we need to discuss what we're doing to move forward. The king is planning something that involves dark magic. Ingrid is trying to undermine me at every turn, and I can't afford to have you two distracted." I fixed my gaze on Oryn, my violet eyes meeting light ones. "I need to know if you can stand against your father when the time comes."

Confusion flashed across Oryn's face as he looked from me to Kyler. "I've never supported his reign. If you require my loyalty, it's yours without question. Everything I have belongs to you. My father's crown, his life, the throne itself—name it and it's yours. I would carve out my own heart and offer it freely if you asked."

"As for the three of us," Kyler interrupted, his voice like gravel, "you don't need to worry about us fighting over you. We can behave."

"We can learn to share, Love." Oryn said, his lips curving into a wicked promise.

The tension in the room shifted, morphing into something drenched with anticipation.

"What if you can't?" The words escaped my lips in a breath, barely disturbing the charged air between us.

Kyler's gaze turned molten as it locked with mine before sliding to Oryn like a caress. "I guess we need to demonstrate just how well we can play nicely," Kyler said, his voice smooth as velvet against my skin.

Oryn lifted the bottle one final time, his throat working as he swallowed, before setting it aside with deliberate care. His heated gaze burned through me, igniting liquid fire in my veins.

"For once," Oryn murmured, "I couldn't agree more."

CHAPTER 39

My head swam pleasantly as I watched my two mates exchange that loaded glance. The alcohol had dulled the sharp edges of my anger from earlier, replacing it with a warm, languid feeling that spread through my limbs.

Oryn rose from his chair first, moving with that fluid grace that never abandoned him, even when drunk. He crossed to the couch where I sat, lowering himself beside me with deliberate slowness.

"Is this alright?" he murmured, his fingers brushing a strand of hair from my face.

I nodded, unable to find my voice as Kyler approached from the other side, the sofa dipping under his weight. I found myself bracketed between them, heat radiating from their bodies.

Oryn's lips found mine first, tasting of the spicy spirits we shared. His kiss was achingly familiar, yet somehow new, as if we were rediscovering each other. His hand cradled my jaw, thumb stroking over my cheek with tender reverence.

When we broke apart, Kyler was there, turning my face toward him. His kiss was different—more demanding, with an edge of restraint that made me want to break it. His fingers tangled in my hair, tugging just enough to tilt my head back.

"Beautiful," Oryn whispered against my neck, his breath hot on my skin as his lips traced a path down to my collarbone.

Kyler's hand slid down my arm, fingers intertwining with mine. "We've got you," he promised, his voice rough with desire.

I closed my eyes as four hands began to explore—Oryn's palm splayed across my lower back, Kyler's fingers tracing patterns on my thigh. Each was deliberate, unhurried, as if they had all the time in the world to memorize every inch of me. Like the world wasn't closing in on us every moment that passed.

Oryn's mouth returned to mine while Kyler's lips found the sensitive spot behind my ear that made me shiver. The contrast of sensations—Oryn's gentle devotion and Kyler's controlled intensity—left me breathless, caught in a current between them.

"I think our greedy mate needs more," Oryn mused.

A dull vibration from Kyler's responding hum tickled my neck.

"I don't think I'm the greedy one between us." I answered.

"I don't see anyone else here having two princes worshipping them, Princess." Kyler said as he lifted me from my spot on the couch, returning me to the bed. The sheets were still in disarray from Oryn and I earlier. "On your knees," he demanded.

I follow his command as Oryn climbed onto the bed before me. He towered over me on his knees, his hands brushing my hair over my shoulder.

"Oh Love, you are absolutely perfect."

My knees were knocked further apart with Kyler's, one hand splaying on my back, pushing me down while the other pulled me back towards him by my hip.

"Open up, Love." Oryn's hand tilted my chin towards him, his cock already hard once again as he readily offered to me. I licked the bead of liquid already accumulating on the tip before allowing him to slide it into my mouth. I tasted myself from our moment earlier, the sensation only adding to the intensity as he started pumping into my mouth.

A pressure from behind began once Ryn caught a steady rhythm. Kyler sheathed himself inside me, his thick length stretching me with the sweetest burn. He gave a moment for my body to adjust to him before he started taking what he wanted, what he needed from me.

"You don't know how badly I wanted to interrupt earlier," he growled as he thrusted into me.

"I think our mate will happily take us both from now on. Won't you, Love?" Oryn replied. I couldn't answer him. My mouth was too full to manage more than a wanton hum. Their words spread a surge of warmth through my body. I moaned around his cock as they both increased in speed. I silently thanked the gods as I got closer and closer to the edge. I took back every qualm I ever voiced over having a mate, let alone two. They were deliciously commandeering, sweet words mixed with filth. Every touch from them lit me on fire in the best way. How did I ever deny they were made for me and I for them?

I tightened around Kyler and took Oryn deeper into my mouth. I was falling fast and needed to drag them with me. Oryn was the first to let go, filling my mouth with his seed. His moans were the final push I needed to crest the wave of pleasure, bringing Kyler to ruin with me. We stayed connected until we collapsed, the soft bedding catching us.

Kyler was the first to get up, going to the ensuite and returning with a damp rag. He gently cleaned between my legs. Once he was finished, Oryn pulled me beneath the plush blankets, nestling me between the two of them. Oryn pressed to my back as I laid my head on Kyler's chest. For the first time in this gilded cage, I felt at peace.

CHAPTER 40

B ut only just for a moment.

My worries returned once again.

I blinked through the haze brought onto me from my pleasure, suddenly remembering something that had slipped past me earlier.

"You knew," I said.

"What's that?" Kyler asked.

I turned to Oryn, who looked just as confused as his friend. "You knew Kyler is a prince," I looked at Kyler, the pieces falling together. "You two have been working together this entire time?"

"Is that so hard to believe?" Oryn asked.

"No," I started, "but that would mean you kept your enemy at your side. How——?"

"I kept to myself for a long time, most forgot Esmeray even has a prince," Kyler answered. "It was the only way to quell some of the unrest, but there's only so much we can do between the two of us. We were never enemies, Lor. We both knew we'd have to be the ones to end this war."

"And the king does not know? Shouldn't he, of everyone, know a neighboring kingdom's heir exists?"

"My father can't be bothered by anything that doesn't serve him. Not once since I brought Kyler on as my right hand has he made any comments. Given his proximity to the throne, it would be treason if he ever found out," Oryn mentioned.

I stared at them, these two princes who had been living double lives, executing their parts while secretly working on a plan of their own.

"I can't believe I didn't see it before," I said, "is that why you never fought against us when we kidnapped you?" I turned to Oryn, "Because you had this alliance with Kyler?"

"I found it pretty alluring. Not only is my wife ruthless, she's good with chains." He winked at me, that sly smirk returning once again.

"You're ridiculous."

"And yet, you love me."

"Anything else you two need to share? There cannot be any more secrets if we're to trust each other." I reminded them.

They shook their heads in unison.

"We couldn't tell you before," Oryn said softly. "It wasn't just our lives at stake and there have been too many ears around."

"I understand," I said, "but you both have me now, and we have a lot of work to do if we're going to stop whatever is coming. I found notes in your father's study... he's been experimenting with my blood. It sounds like he's been able to unlock some sort of power that could lead to utter decimation."

Kyler growled as he pulled me back to his chest. Any gaps between Oryn and me are quickly closed. "We won't let it get that far. We can tail him tomorrow and see what we can find."

I felt Oryn nod behind me.

"I'll send a message to Lucas. Set up a meeting. We'll need any help we can get."

Silence blanketed us once again as the start of our plan fell into place.

"He'll die before he hurts you again, Alora." Oryn whispered so softly I almost didn't hear it. Pain laced in his words, heavy with guilt.

I patted his arm that wrapped around my middle reassuringly.

There was no doubt the king would fall before this was all over, even if I had to sacrifice myself to do it.

CHAPTER 41

I woke before sunrise, my body still pleasantly sore from the night before. My princes were gone, already starting their part of our hastily formed plan. I dressed quickly in a deep blue gown that would help me blend in with the nobles while still allowing my movements the freedom they needed. Moving to Oryn's oak desk, I scribbled a quick note on some spare parchment and sealed the letter into a small envelope.

Since Oryn and Kyler would be trailing the king today, I decided Shefferd would be my target. He knew all of the comings and goings in this place, surely he knew something.

Finding Shefferd wasn't difficult. The man moved through the castle with purpose, his nasally breathing audible before I even turned corners. I kept to alcoves and ducked behind tapestries whenever he glanced back.

He carried a stack of scrolls, occasionally muttering to himself as he checked them against some mental list. When he entered the king's study and emerged empty-handed, I knew I was on the right track.

By midday, my feet ached from the constant movement that was trailing his flittering about the palace. That's when Shefferd's behavior shifted. His hurried pace slowed as he approached an unmarked door in the east wing—a section of the castle rarely used. He glanced around, his beady eyes scanning the corridor before slipping inside.

I crept forward, pressing my ear against the weathered wood.

"Everything proceeds as planned," Shefferd's voice carried through. "The vessel hasn't shown any signs of damage since her return."

There was a pause, as if someone was responding, but I heard nothing.

"Yes, my queen. The sacrifice will be ready by the next solstice."

My blood ran cold. Sacrifice?

You're still getting yourself into trouble, I see. My hallucination of Maël returned once again in a time I didn't need the distraction.

I haven't done a single thing. If anything, it follows me like a plague.

That isn't how I remember our childhood. Seems you should be running away from danger, not towards it.

Great, not only was the figment of my imagination back, but it was treating me like a child.

If I don't stop it, it could hurt someone else.

It does you no good to be so self sacrificing.

Everything takes sacrifice, Maël. You, of all people, should know that.

He didn't deem me worthy of a response as I felt him recede once again.

"The princess consort suspects nothing," Shefferd continued, "her return has actually accelerated our timeline."

I bit my lip to keep from gasping, this was exactly what I didn't want to have happen. Obliviously aiding their plan was not something I could afford.

When his footsteps approached the door, I darted behind a nearby column. Shefferd emerged, locked the door with a key from his pocket, and hurried away.

I waited until his footsteps faded before trying the door. Locked, as I expected. With a quick glance around, I pulled my thinnest dagger from my bodice and shoved it into the mechanism, prying it open with a click.

The room was empty. Completely empty. Not a single piece of furniture, no windows, nothing but bare stone walls. Yet Shefferd had clearly been speaking to someone.

I inspected every inch—running my hands along the walls, checking for hidden passages—but found nothing. It was as if his partner had simply vanished.

With a frustrated sigh, I slipped out, relocking the door. I needed to find Kyler and Oryn, but first I had to establish my alibi. The library would be perfect—I'd told Luella that's where I'd be spending my day.

As I rounded the corner to the grand library, I collided with a solid form.

"Lor!" Davian steadied me with gentle hands. Oryn's younger brother had grown taller since I'd last seen him at our wedding. I barely saw him in passing since my return. I had heard the queen had given him a rigorous tutoring schedule. Now that I was able to get a good look, his boyish features had began to sharpen.

"Davian," I smiled, genuinely pleased to see him. "I'm sorry for running into you."

"I'd been hoping to find you since your return." His eyes lit up. "I've been caring for Raven in your absence. He's missed you terribly."

My heart squeezed at the mention of my steed. "Raven did take to you quite well."

"I wouldn't let anyone else near him. He's been... difficult for others to handle."

I laughed, picturing my temperamental horse terrorizing the stable hands. "I've missed him, too."

"Would you like to see him now?" Davian offered, "I finished my lessons for the day and was just heading to the stables."

This was as good an alibi as any and Oryn and Kyler would still be gone for a bit longer. "Lead the way."

I followed Davian through the castle corridors, my heart quickening with each step closer to the stables. The thought of seeing Raven again filled me with equal parts excitement and guilt.

"He'd nearly bitten off a stable boy's finger last month," Davian said, glancing back at me with a grin. "Father wanted him sold not long after you were taken, but Oryn wouldn't hear of it."

My throat tightened. "And your father listened?"

"Seems like it," Davian shrugged, "he doesn't usually care about such things. But Oryn said you'd never forgive him if he let your horse go, so I volunteered to take care of him. Figured it might earn me some favor with my new sister-in-law."

We stepped into the stables, the familiar scents of hay and leather washing over me. At the far end, in the largest stall, stood a midnight black stallion.

"Raven," I whispered.

His head shot up, ears perked forward. For a moment, he stared at me, unmoving. Then he let out a high-pitched whinny that echoed through the stable.

I rushed to him, ignoring the curious stares of the stable hands. Raven pressed his velvet muzzle against my palm, nickering softly.

"I'm so sorry," I murmured, stroking his neck. "I didn't mean to leave you for so long."

"He was inconsolable for weeks," Davian said, leaning against the stall door. "Wouldn't eat, wouldn't let anyone near him except me and Oryn."

Guilt crashed over me like a wave. I pressed my forehead against Raven's, breathing in his familiar scent. "Thank you for taking care of him."

"He's a magnificent beast. Temperamental, but loyal." Davian handed me an apple. "His favorite."

I offered it to Raven, who took it delicately from my palm. As he munched, I examined him closely. His coat gleamed with health, his muscles strong beneath my hands.

"You've done well by him," I said, genuine gratitude in my voice.

"It was the least I could do," Davian smiled, "especially after you plucked me from that bush. Would you like to take him out? The eastern meadow is beautiful this time of year."

I shook my head reluctantly. "Not today. But soon."

Looking at Raven, I made a decision. He couldn't stay here when everything went to hell. I needed to get him back to the guild before we made our move. Lucas would grumble, but he'd take Raven back for me.

"Is there a messenger available?" I asked casually. "I'd like to send word to my uncle that I've returned safely."

"Of course," Davian replied. "I'll call for one."

I pulled the letter I had written this morning from my pocket. When the messenger arrived, I handed him the sealed note. "For Augustus Denarius at the bookshop in Epherinia. Please deliver it to the door behind the shop."

The young boy nodded earnestly.

I slipped him extra coins. "It would mean a great deal to me."

The coded message would tell Lucas and Rasher everything they needed to know. Tonight, we would meet and set our plans in motion.

"Come," I said to Davian, giving Raven one last stroke. "Let's let him rest."

CHAPTER 42

It wasn't long after I returned to my room that my co-conspirators arrived. Shefferd was the biggest lead we had other than the documents I found in the king's study. Every hour we spent waiting for the night to blanket the land seemed to drag on endlessly.

I fidgeted with the clasp of my cloak, watching Oryn check the corridor for the third time. Kyler stood by the window, his dark silhouette framed against the moonlight as he scanned the grounds below.

"We're clear," Oryn whispered, closing our chamber door. "The guards just changed shifts."

"Before we go," I said, my voice low but firm, "we need to bring Magnus with us."

Both men turned to stare at me.

"Absolutely not," Oryn said.

Kyler's brow furrowed. "That's too risky, Lor."

"He's your most trusted guard," I countered, looking at Oryn. "And he's been watching your father's movements for years. He knows things we don't."

"And if he's loyal to the king?" Kyler challenged.

I shook my head. "I don't believe he is. When he was assigned to me, he swore his sword to me. No other guard on my detail rotation has done the same."

"It's still a gamble," Oryn said, running a hand through his hair.

"A necessary one," I insisted, "we need all the allies we can get. Besides, if we're discovered, he'll be implicated whether he knows our plans or not."

The princes exchanged a look I couldn't quite decipher.

"Fine," Oryn finally conceded. "But if he betrays us—"

"He won't," I said with more confidence than I felt. "If he does, I'll take responsibility."

Within the hour, the four of us slipped from the castle through the servant's exit. Magnus had asked surprisingly few questions when Oryn summoned him, simply nodding when told it was a matter requiring the utmost secrecy.

I wrapped shadows around us as we mounted our horses, cloaking our departure from prying eyes. The darkness moved like smoke, twisting and flowing around our forms.

"Gods above," Magnus muttered as the shadows enveloped Raven, making my stallion's midnight coat absorbed all light. "Your horse looks like a nightmare brought to life."

"He rather enjoys it," I whispered back, patting Raven's neck as he pranced beneath me, untroubled by the darkness.

We rode hard through the sleeping city, keeping to back alleys and deserted streets as Kyler led us to our destination. The bookshop stood dark and silent when we arrived, but I knew better than to assume it was empty.

The moment we slipped through the back door, Lucas launched himself at me, nearly knocking me over with his enthusiastic embrace.

"Finally!" he exclaimed, squeezing me tight before stepping back to examine our companions. His eyes lingered appreciatively on

Rasher, who stood by the hearth with his arms crossed. "Tall, dark, and handsome over there was about to send a search party."

Rasher's expression remained impassive. "We don't have a lot of time for socializing, it won't be long until the townsfolk start rising for the day."

I paced the cramped back room of the bookshop while Lucas spread out a map of the castle on the rickety table. The candles cast long shadows as we gathered around, our faces grim in the flickering light as I recalled everything we knew.

"Shefferd mentioned a vessel and a sacrifice," I said, recounting what I'd overheard. "He said my return accelerated their timeline."

Kyler's jaw tightened. "That fits with what I observed. Your father," he nodded to Oryn, "has been meeting with members of the old faith. Practitioners who worship the lost gods."

"The king has always collected ancient texts," Magnus added, his normally stoic face troubled. "Scrolls from the forbidden archives, he even sent small parties to raid old temples. One of those men made the mistake of reading one during their return journey. Said it spoke of harnessing celestial power through blood sacrifices. Only a few heard of this. He was executed shortly after the return."

"What celestial power?" Oryn asked, leaning forward.

Magnus hesitated. "There are stories... legends about vessels who could channel the power of these gods. They were mere children's tales when I was a young one."

Every eye turned to me.

"Death's Wraith," Rasher murmured, his deep voice breaking the silence.

Magnus' brows drew close. "What does that criminal have to do with this?"

I watched as Oryn and Lucas' eyes met across the table, both of them hiding a snicker. I felt conflicted between the joy of the two of them bonding and the desire to throttle them both for their childishness at a time like this. Maybe later when I wasn't thwarting someone wanting to harvest my blood for power.

"I am Death's Wraith," I admitted, "Death and I are connected somehow, though even after meeting him, I don't really understand it."

Magnus eyes looked to Kyler for confirmation, who solemnly nodded. "There's more to it, but what she's saying is true."

The old guard appraised me with new eyes slowly. It wasn't until our eyes met once again that the silent tension was broken by his chuckle.

"I should've known after that tea party."

I couldn't help but smile, recalling that moment.

Rasher cleared his throat, bringing us back to the present issue. "The king must know what you are, Alora. He's planning to use your connection to Death in some ritual if all of this is to be believed."

I felt sick. "How does he even know what I am?" I whispered, my fingers tracing the outline of Sunneva on the map. "I didn't know it myself until we were face to face with Death."

"The king has always been obsessed with ancient prophecies," Oryn said, leaning against the bookshelf. "But this level of knowledge about the workings of the gods... it's unsettling."

Kyler's eyes met mine across the table. "Someone must have told him. Someone who recognized what you are."

"Elvirana," Magnus said suddenly. We all turned to him. "The royal mage has the ability to sense power within fae, that's why Aurelius employed her. I've seen her test children brought to court, identifying their affinities before they've even manifested."

My stomach twisted. "She assessed me when I first arrived in the capital. Shefferd told me it was required of every maiden in the kingdom."

"It is," Oryn confirmed, "he always spoke about finding me a powerful match, that it was in the best interest of the kingdom. Your assessment was like nothing I had seen in the prior ones."

"We need to question her," Rasher said, "find out exactly what she told the king."

Lucas snorted. "And how do you propose we do that? It sounds like the king keeps her close."

"The masquerade ball," Oryn said, his eyes lighting up. "It's in three days. Every noble in the kingdom will attend, including Elvirana. It may be the only time before the next solstice."

"She never leaves the king's side during court functions," Magnus pointed out.

I tapped my fingers on the table, thinking. "Then we separate them. Create a distraction that forces the king away."

"What if we can't?" Lucas asked, voicing the concern written on all of our faces. "What if we can't get to her?"

Oryn's expression hardened. "Then we'll have to kill him."

The room fell silent. Kyler stared at Oryn, concern etched across his features.

"You'd kill your own father?" he asked.

"Without hesitation," Oryn replied, his voice steady. "Alora will never be safe as long as he lives, if this is what he's planning. I won't let him use her as some weapon to help him achieve his twisted ambitions."

The weight of his words settled over us. For all our differences, for all the pain between us, Oryn was willing to commit regicide to protect me, against his own father no less.

"Magnus?" I asked the old guard.

Magnus didn't hesitate to answer, "my vow to you supersedes any made before you came under my protection. I told myself I would break the one I carried for the king if someone worthy would come. I always thought it would be the prince," he looked to Oryn fondly. "Who would've thought it'd be Death's Wraith."

"Let's hope we can get her alone," I said.

As we prepared to leave, I pulled Lucas aside. "I need you to do something for me."

His eyes lit up. "Anything for you, darling. What sort of secret mission do you have for me?"

"Take Raven back to Vanya's stables. I can't leave him here when everything falls apart."

Lucas' enthusiasm instantly deflated. "You want me to escort your demon horse? The same horse that tried to bite my fingers off the last time I went near him?"

"He likes apples," I offered with an apologetic smile.

"Apples won't save me if he decides to trample me to death," Lucas groaned, "why not send Rasher? He's good with animals."

"Because I need Rasher here. Please, Lucas. I wouldn't ask if it wasn't important."

He sighed dramatically. "The things I do for you. Fine, but you owe me."

CHAPTER 43

The next three days passed in a blur of preparation. Every spare moment was dedicated to plotting our next moves for the masquerade ball. When not attending to my duties, I found myself studying the palace layout, memorizing guard rotations, and practicing the subtle art of court conversation that revealed nothing while extracting everything. We even brought Luella into the fold. Her ability to gather intel without drawing attention to herself proved to be invaluable.

This had to go off without a hitch.

Magnus was instrumental with creating the plan, sharing details about the mage's habits he's observed over the years. Kyler and Oryn set aside their desire to take me to bed every second of the day, long enough to coordinate our approach to Elvirana. Even Lucas, before departing with my reluctant horse, provided me with a set of locksmithing tools, telling me to stop abusing my daggers for such a simple thing.

Rasher, with the help of Luella, established contact with sympathetic servants, creating a network of eyes throughout the palace. Every whisper, every unusual movement was reported back to us through my handmaiden. She was without a doubt our most trusted messenger.

On the morning of the ball, I awoke with dread coiling in my stomach. Oryn had already left our chambers, attending to last minute preparations with his father. Kyler had left earlier to sneak back into his rooms at the barracks, not wanting to draw too much attention to his now frequent overnight visits in our chamber. I spent the day in anxious anticipation, barely touching the food Luella brought.

By evening, Luella arrived with my gown—a creation of blood red silk that flowed like liquid fire. As she helped me dress, I watched the door carefully, ensuring we were truly alone.

"Luella," I said softly as she pinned my hair, "I need you to remember something."

Her hands paused. "My lady?"

"About tonight... if things turn into chaos, I need you to go north."

She met my eyes in the mirror, her brow furrowed. "North? To Bridgedale?"

"Further," I said, "to the northern capital. I need you to take a message to the queen."

"Lady Lor, you're frightening me," Luella whispered, her hands trembling as she placed jeweled pins in my hair.

"It's just a precaution," I assured her, squeezing her hand. "But promise me you'll go tell the queen 'a gilded cage is no place for a wraith'. Promise me you'll remember."

"A gilded cage is no place for a wraith," she repeated. "I promise."

A knock at the door ended our conversation. Oryn entered, fitted in his matching attire, his golden crown nestled among his light waves.

"You look stunning," he said, his eyes sweeping over me appreciatively.

I rose from my seat, feeling the weight of the night ahead. "As do you."

He offered his arm. "Shall we?"

Oryn and I entered the grand ballroom arm in arm, our presence drawing every eye in the room. The symbolism wasn't lost on me—we looked like walking sacrifices, draped in the color of what might soon be spilled.

Remember, Oryn sent through the bond while he smiled and nodded to passing nobles. *I'm right here, Love.*

I squeezed his arm in acknowledgement, plastering on my most dazzling smile.

I know.

The ballroom glittered with hundreds of candles, reflecting off jewels and polished marble. I scanned the crowd, noting Kyler's position near a column, his eyes following our every move while pretending to be engaged in conversation with Magnus. Our gazes met briefly—a flash of connections that sent warmth through our bond before I was forced to look away.

"Your Highness," a nobleman bowed deeply for us. "What a pleasure to see you both looking so... united."

I recognized the subtle probe in his words. Court gossip about our strained relationship now that Oryn had taken a mistress had clearly spread.

"We've never been more united," Oryn replied smoothly, his hand sliding to the small of my back. "My wife and I have always had a special relationship. There's no other I could imagine spending my life with."

I leaned into him, playing my part. "It's not often to find such a love in times like these. I'm so grateful to the gods who brought us together."

We moved through the crowd like this, dancing our verbal dance with each noble we encountered. When the orchestra struck up a waltz, Oryn led me to the center of the floor, his hand firm against mine.

"Elvirana is here," he murmured as we twirled. "Near the eastern archway."

I followed his subtle nod, catching sight of the royal mage in her billowing robes. She stood just off to the side from where the king sat on his throne.

"We need to—"

"May I cut in?" Ingrid appeared beside us. Her golden gown hugged her figure tightly. The gilded dust Luella had used on me before covered almost every inch of her skin. Her smile was sweet, her eyes venomous.

"I'm afraid not," Oryn replied coolly. "I'm rather enjoying this dance with my wife."

Ingrid's smile faltered. She recovered only to gently slide her hands along his arm. "Surely you can spare one dance for an old friend—"

Oryn leaned close to her ear, his voice dropping to a whisper I could barely hear. "Touch me again without permission, and you'll find yourself in the most desolate pit in the desert."

I couldn't help the pleased smile that crept across my face as Ingrid's complexion paled.

"And if I so much as hear about another word against my wife or if you ever attempt at causing her harm," he continued, "I'll have you nailed to the palace walls for the birds to pick at your intestines while you watch."

She retreated without another word, tears forming in her eyes and no doubt spilling before she could flee the room.

"That was satisfying," I admitted as we continued our dance.

Oryn's lips quirked. "I've stopped myself countless times from dragging her to the executioner's block. Kyler wanted to do much worse. Alas, the woes of behaving while lying low."

"You both wanted to harm her?" I asked.

"You're not the only one capable of hurting others, Love." He said, another lavish twirl as the pace picks up. "Seems our girl has corrupted us."

I laughed, not able to picture Kyler ever being corrupted. Oryn, on the other hand...

As the dance ended, I noticed Elvirana slipping through a side door. "She's on the move."

We made our excuses to nearby nobles and followed, maintaining a careful distance. The corridor was dimly lit, perfect for our pursuit. Kyler and Magnus fell in behind us, their footsteps nearly silent.

She appears to be alone. Kyler's voice filled my head, extending to Oryn as well. We tracked her through the winding, unfamiliar hallways.

But as we turned the final corner, I caught sight of another figure joining her—the king himself, his crown gleaming in the torchlight. They entered a chamber together, the heavy door closing behind them.

"This is our chance," I breathed. The rush of the chase coursed with excitement in my veins, but fear still mingled below the surface.

We approached cautiously, listening at the door before Oryn tested the handle. It turned easily—too easily. The room was utterly empty.

"It's a trap," Kyler hissed, but it was too late.

The door slammed shut behind us, locks clicking into place from the outside.

CHAPTER 44

The echo from the door sent ice through my veins. Magnus tried the handle, but it wouldn't budge.

"I knew you were all fools," the king's voice came from behind us, "but I never imagined you'd be this predictable."

We spun around to find him emerging from behind a concealed panel in the wall, flanked by six royal guards with drawn swords. Their armor gleamed in the dim light, those blasted suns stared at us mockingly.

"You led us here," I said, the realization dawning on me like a sickening wave.

The king's smile was serpentine. "Of course I did. Every breadcrumb, every whisper, every bit of mysterious information that was fed to you—all carefully placed for you to find." He spread his hands wide. "And like the desperate fools you are, you followed the trail right into my waiting hands."

Kyler shifted closer to me, his hand hovering near his concealed blade. Oryn stood rigid beside me, his face a mask of cold fury as he stared at his father.

"Your betrayal runs deeper than I imagined," Oryn said, his voice barely above a whisper. "Why? What was the point of all of this?"

"Betrayal?" The king laughed. "I've only ever done what was necessary for Sunneva. Her blood, her power, it'll allow us to conquer every land we set our boots upon. The world will be ours, Oryn. Everyone will bow before us, worshipping us like the sun."

A strange light began to illuminate the room from behind him—an eerie blue glow that pulsed like a heartbeat. The air crackled with energy as the wall behind the king seemed to tear open, revealing a shimmering portal.

Stony guards entered first, only a handful, but enough to circle around me and my friends.

Then a woman stepped through, her movements fluid and graceful. She wore a gown of midnight blue that seemed to absorb the light around her, and atop her head sat a crown of what looked like stone, jagged and beautiful. Her dark hair cascaded down her back, and when she lifted her gaze, I found myself staring into violet eyes that mirrored my own.

My breath caught in my throat.

"Alora," she said, her voice like velvet over steel. "How you've grown. The last time I saw you, you had barely learned to walk."

I couldn't speak, couldn't move. Those eyes—my eyes—studied me with cold calculation.

"Trinity," the king greeted.

"Mother?" I breathed, recognition and shock mingling in my voice.

She smiled, the expression never reaching her eyes. "King Aurelius, thank you kindly for returning her to me. You will be greatly rewarded."

"Of course, Your Highness," the golden king bowed deeply to her.

A scuffle sounded behind me. At a flick of her wrist, one of the stone faced guards shoved Magnus forward, forcing him to his knees before her. He grimaced as she griped his chin with her hand, forcing him to look at her.

"Isn't this lovely?" Trinity said, surveying us all with a predatory satisfaction as she released his face. He was dragged up in a guard's arms, his eyes found mine for just a moment, regret filling them. "My family, finally reunited after all these years. A daughter I abandoned, and a long forgotten lover." Her gaze slid to Kyler, "—and an unexpected addition. How quaint."

My mind reeled, trying to keep up with everything around me. Trinity—my mother? The woman I'd assumed was dead all these years stood before us, radiating power and malice. And Magnus—I risked a glance at the old guard—was he...?

Before I could process this betrayal, Kyler lunged forward, daggers flashing in the dim light. "Now!" he shouted.

Chaos erupted.

Kyler slammed into the first guard, driving his blade up through the gap in his armor. The guard didn't scream, didn't even flinch, just stared with those vacant eyes.

I drew my blade, darkness curling around my fingers as I faced two guards advancing on me.

Magnus broke free from his captor's grip, sweeping the man's legs and stealing his sword in one fluid motion.

Oryn's fire burst to life, golden flames encircling his hands as he engaged the remaining guards.

"Take them alive!" Trinity commanded, her voice cutting through the clash of steel. "I need the girl!"

The king backed away, slipping behind the fray towards the door. "This wasn't the plan," he hissed at her. "You said my son would remain with me, that you didn't have need of him."

"Plans change," she replied, cold and dismissive.

I ducked beneath a guard's blade, slashing across his hamstring. He stumbled but didn't fall—didn't even bleed. What were these things?

"They're not alive!" Magnus shouted, driving his sword through a guard's chest. The creature, who looked like a guard, kept fighting, the blade lodged in its torso.

Oryn's fire engulfed one of the guards, revealing stone-like skin beneath melting flesh. "Golems!" he yelled. "They're constructs!"

Elvirana appeared at the king's side, her hands weaving complex patterns as she muttered incantations. The air grew thick with magic.

"Retreat!" Trinity commanded the remaining guards. "Bring me my daughter!"

Three guards broke from the fight, lunging toward me with unnatural speed.

Kyler saw them coming. "Alora, duck!"

I dropped as he vaulted over me, tackling two guards at once. The third caught me by the arm, its grip like iron as it dragged me toward the portal.

"No!" I twisted, driving my dagger into its eye. The creature didn't release me.

Oryn appeared at my side, burning through the golem's arm with concentrated fire. The limb crumbled to ash, freeing me.

Trinity stepped backward into the portal. "Seize the girl! Now!"

The remaining guards converged on me. Magnus and Oryn fought desperately to keep them at bay, but they were overwhelming us.

One caught my ankle, another my wrist. They pulled me toward the swirling vortex of energy.

"Alora!" Kyler shouted, breaking free from his opponents. He sprinted toward me, eyes wild with determination.

The guards yanked me forward. The portal's energy crackled against my skin.

Kyler reached me in a final desperate lunge, pulling me backward with all his might. I stumbled into Oryn's arms as Kyler, without missing a beat, lunged forward, tackling the guards.

"No!" I screamed as my mate, in his attempt to keep the guards away from me, had hurled himself into the portal. All I saw was a tangle of limbs as the entrance to the portal started to shrink. Our eyes locked for one heartbreaking moment before the swirling energy swallowed him whole.

The portal had begun to collapse, its light fading.

I lunged forward, but Magnus and Oryn caught me, pulling me back.

"Kyler!" I screamed, fighting against their grip. "Let me go! We can't leave him!"

"The portal's collapsing," Magnus grunted, dragging me toward the exit. "We'll all die if we stay!"

I'd gladly sacrifice myself for him. For any one of them.

"We'll find him," Oryn promised, his voice breaking as he pulled me from the chamber. "Alora, we'll find him."

The last thing I saw was the portal winking out of existence, taking Kyler with it.

*The harbinger of flame will cleanse
this land, will save us all.*

ORYN POV BONUS

Do you want to experience the night Alora met Oryn from his point of view? What if it had a little bit of...spice? Subscribe to my newsletter to gain access to that fateful night in the tavern from Oryn's perspective, including where he went that next morning.

ACKNOWLEDGMENTS

I never thought I'd be releasing this only six months after releasing the first. I hate to parrot my previous acknowledgments, but I sit here in utter disbelief that I've published not one, but two books in the most insane year of my life. There were a lot of really big changes that happened for me and my family. But through it all Alora's story still spoke to me.

I wanted to thank the amazing artists who made this project absolutely beautiful: INK Designs, Paige Annabentleah, and Valery Maroushchak. You each have a gift with bringing the vision to life in the most spectacular way.

My dearest of friends Erin Archer, my soul sister and the best writing partner I could have ever asked for. Words could never express how grateful I am that we met and have chosen to travel this journey together. Being an author is is fun, but experiencing it with you has made it all the better. Thank you for thriving in the chaos with me.

A special thank you to my friend and neighbor Bree, you've helped me push past my own internal boundaries that I would have let hold me back for years. Your feedback has been invaluable and I appreciate your insight on all things bookish. I'm so glad we met in Mrs. Knight's class.

A big thank you to my street team: Janai, Bree, Renee, and Monika. I appreciate each and every one of you and I couldn't be more honored to have you on the team.

Thank you to my Beta & ARC readers, you have no idea how

grateful I am to have you take a chance on me and I hope you enjoyed Princess of Flames and Fate as much as I enjoyed writing it.

To my friends and family, thank you for your never ending support.

My beautiful daughters Téylie & Isla, thank you for being pure sunshine. You both keep things interesting in the best, most chaotic way possible and I love every second of it.

To my husband Sam, I know you were pretty upset with me for Maël after how closely you identified to him, little did you know you've inspired every male lead I've ever and will ever write. You're the best man I know and I couldn't imagine experiencing life with anyone else. You are the soul forever entwined with my own.

BLIND BITE: A BEST FANGS FOREVER NOVELLA

Read on for a first look at my new series Best Fangs Forever: a paranormal romance with a dash of romcom about two best friends navigating love, college, careers, and the endless possibilities of eternity. Blind dates suck & love bites.

CHAPTER 1

LILITH

"No! You don't love him, he's manipulating you with empty promises." I flung popcorn towards the TV that cast a blue glow across my living room. *Love Village*, my favorite reality TV show, played while I cuddled on the couch with my sweet cat, Mysti. "Sarah, you're way too good for that narcissist." The kernels bounced off the screen with tiny pings as I continued my assault in frustration.

I slid off the couch and scooped up my mess before Mysti could consume the buttery goodness. She watched intently as I snatched each piece from under her nose.

"Ugh, stupid. Just stupid." My mind reeled as I tossed all of the popcorn in the trash and turned to face the TV once again to see Sarah smiling brightly at this jerk. This show was my guilty pleasure. Not only is the drama at an all time high with each episode, but the leaks on social media really gave each person some depth. Sarah was my favorite contestant this season, and I really wanted her to find love, but she kept falling for this tool of a guy, Chad, instead of the sweet musician who had more green flags than anyone else there. Reality TV is a cesspit, at least that's what Amelie, my best friend and roommate, always said when she caught me watching it. I've taken to catching up while she's at work to avoid her teasing, thanks to our opposite schedules.

My phone pinged and I looked down to see her name flash on my screen with a text. My stomach dropped as I remembered what day it was.

AMELIE
Are you ready for your date???

LILITH
Ugh, is it too late to say I'm sick or have a paper due?

Yes! Lacey said he was super nice. How often do you get to go on a blind date that has someone like Lace talking about how great they are? She's such a hater! I love that bitch.

Since Lacey pressured me into accepting this blind date, I've been dreading it. Her sales pitch rung in my ears: "He's so sweet. He's artsy just like you! I bet you two would look so cute together. Plus, it totally seems like he showers."

I should've known something was off when our friend, who criticizes everyone and everything—she once spent two weeks shaming me for wearing heels with jeans—suddenly became someone's biggest cheerleader. Honestly, this is the same woman who once wrote a three-page critique of my coffee brewing technique. For her to actually praise someone? Major red flag.

LILITH
If he ends up being a serial killer, don't let my mom see my kindle history.

AMELIE
Nah, I'm keeping that for myself.

Crap, my first class for the morning was in thirty minutes and I was still in my pajamas, wearing my favorite worn-out Sailor Moon sleep shirt and shorts. The university was a twenty minute walk. I scrambled to my room, tossing clothes aside as I reached my closet, clothes flying in every direction. There's no time for a shower and I had work right after my second class. I yanked a skirt and a sweater from the hangers and wrestled them over my bra and panties. Racing out of my room, I stumbled on my boots lying near my door. I barely caught myself on my door frame as I fell. Time was of the essence though so I leapt into our little shared bathroom. My reflection showed my rumpled state. Lavender hair escaped the messy bun I had thrown it up in before bed last night. I pulled my hair out of the band and brushed out the tangles. I scrubbed my teeth quickly and sprayed deodorant everywhere to stay fresh for the day. Who needed body odor?

After I swept black eyeliner above my lashes and put on a little blush and lip gloss, I checked myself out one last time. My vivid hair color always drew attention, but I loved it too much to care what my date might think. Lavender was my favorite, and it felt more right than my natural brown hair. I fixed my oversized evergreen sweater so it dropped off one shoulder, showcasing the little stars tattooed across the space and tucked the front into my black leather skirt. This would have to do, and I needed to leave like five minutes ago.

I returned to my room and pulled on my boots. Mysti sat on my bed near my bag as I scooped my laptop into it and patted her on the head.

"I'll be back later, pretty girl!" I cooed as I made my way out of the apartment, locking our front door behind me.

I stepped out on the street, brick buildings towering along our block. It wasn't student housing, but the next best thing in an affordable neighborhood. I rushed down the road, looking down at my phone and calculating my chances of making it on time. With every cross walk stop, I thought about my blind date later. Could this be the one? Lacey did say this guy was nice and 'one of the good ones', whatever that meant. But what did she really know? They'd only worked on some class projects together.

It didn't seem like she knew him all that well, but seemed pretty sure we would hit it off. When she first brought him up, I waved her off, not taking it very seriously. But she persisted and finally got me interested enough to give the go-ahead to pass along my number. Only instead of doing that, she set up this whole blind date. Thanks to Amelie, she knew my schedule enough to find a time that worked for both of us. I didn't even know the guy's name, but I was meeting him at a restaurant near my work.

Butterflies fluttered in my stomach as I finally made it to campus. I've always wanted to fall in love, and many times I did, only for it to go wrong. I've had too many dates turned into boyfriends that quickly fizzled out. Was it me? Amelie was adamant it wasn't, but how could one be sure?

Racing to the second building to my left, I grabbed the heavy handle and pulled it open, the hinges let out a loud groan. Maybe this date wouldn't be so bad. Maybe Lacey would be right and this time things would end up working out. I'd finally find my happily ever after just like in all the fairytales.

Thankfully, my classroom was the first in the building as I slid in a minute before the class started. I grabbed the nearest seat, my earlier anxiety settled into nervous excitement.

Also by Ember Johnson

<u>Araceli's Blade Trilogy</u>

Daughter of Shadows and Ash

Princess of Flames and Fate

Queen of Stars and Wrath

<u>Best Fangs Forever</u>

Blind Bite

About the Author

Ember Johnson was born in California where she spent most of her days reading. Naturally, she developed into a book dragon and is currently working on a book collection to rival her grandfathers. She lives in Alabama with her daughters, husband, and beloved pets.

instagram.com/author.emberjohnson

tiktok.com/@author.emberjohnson

threads.net/@author.emberjohnson

goodreads.com/emberjohnson